CW00923668

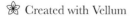

Editing: Lori White Creative Editing Services

Cover Design: Dar Albert, Wicked Smart Designs

Proofreaders: Melinda Kaye Brandt and JT Farrell

❀ Created with Vellum

TO LOVE A THIEF

AN ENEMIES TO LOVERS STEAMY ROMANTIC SUSPENSE

RELENTLESS PURSUIT

DELTA JAMES

My 100th Book—What a ride
it has been! I want to thank each and every
one of you who is reading this book—whether it
is your first or hundredth—
from the bottom of my heart
for allowing me into your life and
allowing me to live my best life and
make my dreams come true.
Your support has, does and will continue
to mean the world to me.
Always,
Delta

This book, as all the rest, is dedicated to
My Two Best Friends:
Renee and Chris, without whom none of
what I do would be possible and to the Girls,
who bring joy to my life every single day.

Acknowledgements As Always to My Team:
Editor: Lori White, Creative Editing Services

Cover Design: Dar Albert, Wicked Smart Designs
Proofreader: Melinda Kaye Brandt

And Special Thanks to Autumn, Kathy,
Maggie, Melinda, and TJ

PROLOGUE

Anything worth stealing when left unprotected or forgotten,
can be stolen away by a thief in the night.

Seamus O'Donnell

CHAPTER 1

CLAIRE

*T*hieves are an entity unto themselves. They have their own subcultures with their norms and customs, and those who run afoul of them often find themselves dead. Had her parents done something so contrary to the honor of the great jewel thieves of the world that someone had decided they needed to die?

To this day, Claire Mitchell found driving on a rainy night an unnerving experience. Given that she routinely climbed or descended from great heights risking imprisonment or death, that was saying something. Even now, as an adult, Claire had to grip the steering wheel tightly in order to keep her hands, normally steady as a rock, from trembling once the raindrops began to fall as the gathering gloom of night descended. It didn't matter that she'd been thrown free of the vehicle still strapped in her car seat. When her parents had perished after their car had been forced from the road, down an embankment and had burst into a fiery inferno, her life had changed forever.

There were nights she could still hear the crackle of the fire and the groan of twisted metal. She could feel its heat and remember the rain as it fell on her face. The doctors told her grandfather, Poppi, that she couldn't remember such things—that she was far too young—but she and Poppi knew better. It had been Poppi who had been there to hold her in his strong arms, to sing the songs of his Irish ancestors, to croon to her in Gaelic and rock her until the trembling and tears faded away.

The moon was ascending to its zenith. It was still the early hours of the night. Those most likely to succumb to either drink or the call of an illicit love affair had found their spot and would be wallowing in their revelries. Claire had found these hours before the moon had fully arisen to be the best time to ply her trade as a master jewel thief. But tonight, she had other plans for the hour closest to midnight. She needed to be done and gone from this job before then.

The Dumar family was on their annual pilgrimage to Corfu, which left their palatial flat in Knightsbridge woefully and inadequately guarded against someone with Claire's talents—well, Claire and her best friend Mia. The penthouse had been lavishly designed by the internationally famous, at least according to her website, Melania Valmar, and was over four thousand square feet. It encompassed the entire top floor of the building and was connected via private, direct access to the lobby that boasted both a concierge and a doorman. The furnishings were a bit much for Claire's taste, but to each their own.

The Dumars had spent an inordinate amount of money on the flat when they acquired it, ensuring it had all the necessary bells and whistles to impress their snooty friends. The problem was they had gone cheap in the wrong areas—their alarm system being one. Not only had she been able to access the elevator shaft via the underground parking garage, accessing their private car, and using the emergency exit in the ceiling to get to the cables which she shimmied up, their alarm bypass code had been ridiculously simple.

For most jewel thieves the riches from which to pick would have been far too many, but Claire always had a goal. There was always one necklace, one pair of earrings, or one bracelet she was after—for Claire wasn't just a master jewel thief, she was a master jewel thief with a cause—to restore to those from whom the 'haves' of this world had stolen what was rightfully theirs.

A chance meeting at the opening of a new, special exhibition at the Metropolitan Museum of London had introduced her to Elisabeth Walton. Claire had been there to scope out any differences between the blueprints she had obtained and the building itself. Both she and Elisabeth had been studying a pearl and diamond choker worn famously by a member of the royal family. Ms. Walton had been enchanting and endearing in the way only proper ladies of London could be. Impulsively, Claire had invited her to high tea the following day at the world-renowned Savoy Hotel. Over tea, Claire had listened with rapt fascination to stories of Ms. Walton's life.

"All in all, my dear, it's been a wonderful life. I've lived through some of the most exciting decades. I was a young woman during the turbulent and fabulous sixties and seventies. It seemed everything that was interesting and fun for a young woman was happening either here or in San Francisco. One of the things Clark had promised we would do was ride the cable cars to Fisherman's Wharf. I always thought that looked like so much fun."

"Clark?" Claire asked.

The old woman's eyes had grown misty. *"Yes. Clark Dumar. We were madly and scandalously in love."*

Claire poured more tea, "Scandalously?"

Elisabeth's eyes twinkled. *"Oh, my, yes."* Claire caught a glimpse of the young woman Elisabeth must have been. She leaned in conspiratorially. *"His family disapproved of the heir to the Dumar fortune falling for one of the shop girls at Harrods."*

"The heart wants what the heart wants."

She chuckled. *"You're still young enough to believe that and the old adage of love conquering all. I suppose both can be true if you both have the requisite strength to follow through."*

"Can I ask what happened?"

Elisabeth sat back, patting Claire's hand before snagging a rhubarb and custard tartlet and popping it into her mouth. "His parents forbade him to see me again and threatened to cut him off without a penny. He said they were furious he had given me the Dumar Diamond—a fabulous necklace of rubies and diamonds with an enormous oval diamond dangling from the center. It made that pearl and diamond thing at the exhibit pale in comparison. He didn't have the courage to build a life with me without the cushion of his family's money. I'm afraid I called him a coward."

"Well, he was."

"No. Just a young man who'd been coddled by his parents' wealth. I have always regretted those were my last words to him."

"What happened to him? Did he marry the girl his parents thought was 'appropriate?'"

"How I wish. No, Clark took his own life. His parents sent the police to retrieve the necklace from me later that day. I wouldn't have kept it."

"Why not? He gave it to you. Obviously, he wanted you to have it."

"I think he probably gave it to me on impulse and that part of what drove him to kill himself was not wanting to face his father's wrath at having done so, or mine for having to retrieve it."

"Do you know what happened to the necklace?"

"Yes. It was in all the papers. His mother said it was 'cursed' and had brought nothing but misfortune to the family. His father vowed to lock it away and never let it see the light of day again."

Claire didn't believe in curses, but she did believe in what was right. She recalled her grandfather having mentioned the scandal and the necklace. Only he had offered that perhaps Clark hadn't killed himself but that a killer had rather had his murder made to look like suicide. Her Poppi had said the old man had been livid not only about the affair, but about Clark having given the necklace to Elisabeth. And when the old man had come to his senses, the family had moved to cover it all up.

She tended to believe Poppi as the backstairs staff usually had the inside scoop on what had actually transpired. From the rumors, Claire knew that Elisabeth had downplayed what had followed Clark's death. The police had been sent to arrest her. They had torn her small flat apart looking for the valuable necklace. It was only after they could find nothing that she was told she could be released with no charges pressed and no record of the incident in exchange for the return of the necklace.

Claire shook her head. There was no way they could have made those charges stick—even if the crown prosecutors had been willing to proceed. Too many staff members and friends of Clark Dumar had known the truth. Elisabeth had never married, preferring to believe Clark had been the one and only great love of her life. Poppycock. Clark Dumar had wanted Elisabeth to have the damn necklace and Claire meant to see that she got it. It would make her remaining years comfortable, but Claire feared Elisabeth would hold it close and leave it to her sister's family when she passed.

Claire looked around the room; the Dumars might have money, but neither they nor their fancy designer had any taste. The furnishings bordered on —no, check that were, in fact, downright gaudy. It was over-the-top ornate and looked more like a red velvet cordoned off section of some royal apartment rather than a place where people lived and breathed. Claire's past made it so the thought of living like that made her want to throw up in her mouth.

Within the community of jewel thieves, the Dumar Diamond Necklace was spoken of with reverence, but no one dared to take it. There were many who believed the necklace was cursed. Claire didn't believe that, not even for a minute.

With Mia's help, getting in and getting to the necklace had been frightfully easy. It wasn't arrogance that made Claire believe she could steal the damn thing; she knew she was among the best that ever lived. Her Poppi had told her that and he never lied— well, except about the whole having been a master thief himself, only Poppi hadn't stolen things to sell or to keep because he found them to be beautiful as any work of art. She smiled, ruefully. No Poppi had been on a mission. He meant to put things right that should never have gone wrong. *I guess the apple didn't fall too far from the tree.*

Mia was in her ear. "Claire? Claire? Are you with me? Look alive, girlfriend. We haven't got all night for this little add-on Robin Hood adventure of yours. You still need to change and get to the Metropolitan Museum of London. This is the last night of the exhibit, and it's a charity fundraiser. You only have three hours to get there and snatch the damn thing. If you miss, there is no 'do over.'"

"You're always so formal. Most people call it the Met. And we could always follow it back to Paris…."

"Oh, hell, no. We are not, I repeat, not, going to take on that cursed *Chateau des Templiers* again. I'd rather try to rob the *Louvre* at gunpoint in the middle of the day. Get moving. If they catch you, Elisabeth will never have her pearls to clutch to her chest."

"They're diamonds, Mia."

"Whatever, Claire. Get your ass in gear."

Claire swung the large Gainsborough landscape away from the wall on its hidden hinge, revealing the safe with its simple keypad lock. She shook her head. The Dumars were idiots—spending all this money on ugly furnishings only to install a safe that a ten-year-old could open. Perhaps not any ten-year-old, but certainly Claire could have done it by that age. The safe's door slid open, and she scooped the necklace into the black velvet bag. Something at the back of the safe caught her eye and she lifted a pearl necklace out, stifling a gasp as she did so.

"Claire? What is it? Are you all right?"

"Yes. I'm holding the Yamamoto Rope. Holy shit," she exclaimed as she lifted a bracelet of diamonds, onyx, and gold in the shape of a leopard. "The Kimani Leopard."

"And you would be rifling through the Dumar's things because?"

"Because they don't belong to the Dumars, or at least they shouldn't." Claire lifted out four pieces she could easily identify as having been stolen—some of them by the Nazis during World War II. "This bugger has a whole cache of stolen jewels."

"Let's not get greedy."

"I'm not. If he notices, the only one he'd report is the Dumar Diamond. The rest would be easily recognizable as stolen. No way he's going to report their theft to the cops."

"Claire!"

"I know, Mia. I'm going; I'll be in the elevator shaft in a couple of minutes."

She tried to walk away—she really did, closing and rearming the alarm for the safe and turning her back on it several times, only to turn back around. In the end, she just couldn't. She scribbled a note on a piece of monogrammed stationery she found in the Louis XIV desk, which read:

I know what you did.
I left you most of your ill-gotten gains.
Shame on you. If the world ever finds out,
you will be ruined.

Realizing Mia was right and that she was running out of time, Claire used a piece of tape she found in the desk drawer and taped it on the face of the safe before swinging the Gainsborough back into place.

Running to the elevator shaft, she slipped through the opening and made a controlled descent back down to the top of the car, back through the escape hatch, landing lightly on her feet, and out into the garage, which had no CCTV cameras either within it or at its entrance. Retrieving her backpack from atop one of the exposed pieces of ductwork in a darkened corner behind a pillar, Claire unzipped her bodysuit and pulled out the pieces of jewelry she'd stuffed down her bra. She made her way up to the street and headed away from the building, keeping her head tucked down to make identifying her from the CCTV footage difficult if not impossible.

She'd need to do some research to find the owners in order to restore the pieces to them. Well, that wasn't precisely true; she'd have Mia do the research.

"Are you out of the Dumars' building?" asked Mia through the commlink.

"It isn't their building."

"Don't argue semantics with me. I'm so glad you're having a good time. I'm on my second Pepto Bismol smoothie of the night."

"Mia, sweetie, I wish you wouldn't get so upset. I've never even been questioned, and the only person who has ever accused me of something was Evangeline Robbins, and no one believed her. We only know someone said something because of that DCI you used to date."

"Ah, Dickie Evers…" Mia sighed.

"Don't take that tone with me. You said he kissed like a dead fish and was lousy in the sack. So, buck up, buttercup. After we're through we'll head to Monte Carlo and live it up."

"I swear you're going to be the death of me," said Mia as Claire slipped into the nondescript van.

"Only if you plan to die having too much fun."

With a wry grin, Mia shook her head. "We've got a glitch in the Grenadine Necklace job."

"What kind of glitch?"

"The insurance company has asked that at the close of tonight's fundraising event that the necklace be pulled from public display and returned to Paris. They plan to have armed guards remove it from the case and walk it out to the armed elevator down to the secure parking lot, into an armored truck and then to a private airport to be taken back to Paris via a private plane."

"Shit. I want that necklace."

"It's worth a small fortune and the insurance company was iffy about allowing the Petacci family to exhibit it at all."

"Rightfully so. It doesn't belong to them."

"No one has ever been able to prove that the Grenadine Necklace didn't find its way into the family long before Clara."

"Knowing and being able to prove are entirely two different things, which is why no one has ever been able to wrest it from their greedy grasp until now."

"You know, if it wasn't for the fact that you don't so much as keep a dime from these heists, I would have left you twisting in the wind in Dusseldorf. But like it or not, you, my friend, are on the side of the angels. I think you're going to have to chalk the Grenadine Necklace up to a loss."

"No. We've put in too much time…"

"And if we get caught?"

"We won't. Let me think a minute." Claire brought her fist up toward her face, bouncing the back of her thumb on her lips.

"While you're coming up with something, you should know, I think someone may be on to us."

"Why do you say that?"

"When I was running my routine this afternoon,

the program found two clandestine hits against our firewall at specific enough times that I don't believe they were random. The first one was the day before the last job in Milan; I might have written that one off to an anomaly. But the second one was just this morning. I think someone is phishing."

Claire looked at Mia and smiled. "It's not like you to just dump a big problem in my lap. What are you thinking?"

"You know me too well," she said with an impish grin. "There is a small—a very small—chance that you still might be able to snatch the necklace. Their plan is to send it out with armed guards who will exit via the still under construction new gallery. Their thinking is that it's wide open, and no one can sneak up on them…"

"But you know better." Despite what Mia liked to tell herself, she got just as much of a buzz out of pulling off these capers as Claire.

"I do. There's a small piece of ducting that runs from the women's loo. We take a canister with knock-out gas and roll it down to them. The loo is right around the corner from the new gallery. Once their down, you slip in, grab the thing and then walk out with the rest of the people at the fundraiser."

Claire returned Mia's wicked smile. "I like it. Simple, elegant, and no one gets hurt. And who will I be this evening?"

"Luckily, it wasn't invitation only. Tickets were

offered exclusively to those who made the right donation…"

"I take it you made the right donation?"

Mia nodded. "Several months ago, just as a backup. I didn't pick up the ticket until a few hours ago. I didn't want us on any lists unless we had to be. There are people who are supposed to attend who know your real name, so I used it for the ticket."

"I'll try to avoid them if I can. In and out, right?"

"That's the order of the day, go in and mingle until just before the end of the party, grab the necklace, and get out. I have your invitation; that sparkly, slinky, stretchy knit evening gown of yours and that very cool tiara we picked up in Tokyo."

"It's not a tiara. It's a headband."

"Whatever. If anyone tries to get a picture of your face, they're screwed."

"If I work it right, it'll never come in to play."

Claire slid into the back of Mia's tech van. In the beginning, Mia had remained at her place in the posh neighborhood of Chelsea, but as Claire had grown bolder, so had Mia. Now, she met Claire wherever they were planning to pull a heist with her tricked-out van whose communication system could probably rival NORAD's.

She removed her clothing and then stepped into the evening gown. She'd purchased it because while beautiful and slinky, it was also very stretchy and did little to inhibit her movement. Using the mirror Mia had provided, Claire reapplied her make up, then quickly tamed her curls so that they would fall past her shoulders, held back by the sparkly electronic headband.

Once she added the headband, she looked straight into one of their cameras and smiled. When she played it back there was a very fashionably dressed lady and where her head should be—nothing but a glowing halo of unrecognizable angelic perfection.

Claire slid back into the passenger seat. "Nobody will be able to see my face or identify me." She said with a smile as she took a last look in the visor mirror and smiled, tucking a set of forensic baffling gloves into her clutch purse along with the small vial of knock-out gas. "Let me off in the alley two blocks away."

As instructed, Mia pulled into an alley and let Claire out. "Be careful. I know this is important to you, but it isn't worth an extended prison sentence. I promise if we don't get it tonight, we'll find another way. I know the tiara thingy will obscure your face, but, if at all possible, avoid the cameras. No need for them to know it's a woman they're looking for."

Claire smiled. "I'll be careful, I promise, but either way, no one is going to see this beautiful face, the heist, or us making the perfect getaway."

CHAPTER 2

CLAIRE

*C*laire walked toward the entrance and handed her ticket to the woman at the reception desk, who handed her a name badge. As she walked away, Claire added it to her clutch. Despite knowing her own skill level and nerves, she never started any job without a slight case of the jitters. They were easily controlled by reminding herself that over the past decade, she had perpetrated more than two dozen high-end jewelry heists. She had dedicated herself to returning the stolen property to its rightful owners and doing so with style and panache.

They say ignorance is bliss, and Claire couldn't disagree. She'd always seen her grandfather through the eyes of an adoring child. Finding out he was somehow involved in the theft of high-end jewelry when she was in her late teens had shaken her to her very core. She'd taken a piece that she knew belonged to a neighbor and simply mailed it to a friend in Dublin and asked her to put the addressed and stamped envelope into the post for her—no questions asked. Claire had always known Mia would never betray her.

At first, finding different and clever ways to return the jewelry she'd found hidden under the floorboard in Poppi's bedroom had been relatively easy. When she was home on a break at the Swiss boarding school she'd been attending, she'd steal into his bedroom when he was out in the stable and thought her asleep —but his cache continued to grow. It appeared he didn't even do anything with the things he stole— simply stashed them away. Maybe it was an addiction of sorts for him; she didn't know. Her trying to redress what she thought were her grandfather's sins came to a screeching halt when he caught her removing a piece of jewelry from his cache.

"What the bloody hell do ye think yer doin'?" he'd asked her angrily. "Those things don't belong to you."

"They don't belong to you, either," she'd responded coolly.

"Nor did they belong to those I took them from."

"Their rightful owners?"

"Not even close. Every single one of those items was taken from their rightful owners, usually violently. I track them down and get them back to them that was stolen from."

"What? You think you're freaking Robin Hood?"

Poppi laughed. "Nah, darlin'. That was a rich man's son robbing his father's enemies and giving it to those who had nothing. I find things that were stolen from their rightful owners by greedy, evil men and see that they get returned to those they rightfully belong to, or at least to their descendants."

She lifted a glittering butterfly brooch from the hole. "Lady Haversham's broach—the one her father gave her. I know I returned it to her…"

Poppi laughed. "And almost gave your poor ole granddad a heart attack when I saw her wearing it again. You do know she never reported it stolen—either the first time or this time."

Claire sat back and crossed her legs, knowing there was a piece of the puzzle she was missing. "Why? They'd need a police report to file an insurance claim."

"You are absolutely right. But when you and your lord husband both know that there is no way to prove the provenance of the piece, you only trot it out for the yokels and never speak of where it came from."

"Where?" Claire asked, fascinated.

"One of the concentration camps. Some of those who came upon them first helped the prisoners inside, but also helped themselves to the gold, jewelry, and other valuables they found there."

"Her brooch?"

Poppi nodded. "Kamp Vaught in the Netherlands. They didn't have a gas chamber, but they did have an execution site with mass graves. Haversham's father and his cronies took the only thing those people had left. I watched 'em do it, and when I reported it up the chain of command, I got cashiered out of the army for my trouble."

Remembering her grandfather always served to steady her nerves. He had endowed her with so much, every bit of knowledge he'd learned from the back-streets of Belfast through the war that was supposed to end all wars, to becoming an unparalleled master thief, surpassing his abilities and allowing him to retire in comfort. Poppi had lived long enough to see her pick up the mantle of his cause and make it her own.

"Now, remember," said Mia via their comm link. "Make sure you're seen but not remembered. I've hacked into their video coverage. Try and keep your face turned away. Head for the ladies loo when they remove the necklace from the case and start to take it away. I'll let you know when they're in position, and you can roll the canister down the air duct."

There wasn't anything Claire could say without calling attention to herself by talking to no one. Best to get a mocktail and mingle. She smiled to herself. Who would have thought that the granddaughter of the horse master and chauffeur to Sir Godfrey Robbins would find herself among the social elite and nobility of London and be perfectly at home as she planned to snatch the Grenadine Necklace right from under their very noses.

Sir Godfrey was a venture capitalist known as much for his ruthlessness as his wealth. He had acquired a palatial estate outside the city of London that rivaled the famed Leeds Castle. Although Godfrey Manor wasn't technically a castle, it was a magnificent manor house situated on over one hundred acres of finely manicured lawns, lush pastures, and glorious English gardens.

Claire had grown up as the poor church mouse cousin to Sir Godfrey's daughter, the glorious Evangeline. Perfect, stunning, unobtainable and every bit as cruel and heartless as her father. Claire and Poppi had lived in a quaint carriage house located between the stables and the garage. As far as Claire was concerned, it had been the perfect childhood.

She glanced around at all the beautiful people— mingling, sipping champagne, delicately nibbling at passing *hors d'oeuvres*, and trying to convince themselves and each other that their being here tonight mattered. It didn't. What mattered was their donations. The fundraiser was merely an elaborate and expensive thank you. Better they spend the hundreds of thousands of dollars on the actual cause than to placate the egos of those who ought to give because they could.

Her role required her to play the part—to be seen in all the right places with all the right people, while she plotted how to liberate their ill-gotten gains from them. Who'd have thought that the chubby tomboy who liked nothing better than to ride horses and run around in breeches, one of her grandfather's sweaters that smelled of his pipe tobacco, and a pair of riding boots would be just as at home mingling with the rich folk her grandfather had despised. Claire didn't despise them—not all of them. Most she sort of pitied as they were never tested to find what they were made of. She found freedom on the back of a horse. On the back of a horse, it didn't matter if you were one of the haves or have nots. All that mattered was ability, nerves of steel, and the horse beneath you.

"Claire, right in front of you... there's a photographer coming straight at you. If he gets a shot of you, he's going to figure out you have the device. Get out of there," whispered Mia in her ear.

Claire spun on her heel, intending to walk away. She needed to be clear of the photographer and to keep him from catching even a glimpse of her. She headed to stand by one of the pillars in the great hall to study the Grenadine Necklace—a stunning piece consisting of a four-strand diamond choker, held together by an exquisite, oval-shaped pink diamond from which a flawless white pear-shaped diamond hung. Claire didn't even want to think about its monetary worth. What was important was that it had come into the hands of fascist dictator Mussolini, who had bestowed it on his mistress, Clara Petacci. Somehow Clara's turncoat cousin, who had been among those on the firing squad as they riddled her body with bullets, had managed to extract it from the hidden pocket in the hem of her skirt before they'd hung her and her lover upside down for the crowd to see.

The necklace had never belonged to the Petacci family—not then, not now. Claire had tracked down a distant relative of the woman to whom it had once belonged and from whom it was taken when she was murdered trying to escape the Nazis via a small fishing boat out of Italy. The woman would never know who had restored the necklace to her family. But Claire would ensure not only that she received it, but also that she had the provenance to prove it rightfully belonged to her.

As she tried to duck behind the pillar in order to put it between her and the photographer, she clumsily ran into a tall, muscular man in an ill-fitting and probably rented tuxedo. He had to be close to six feet, six inches tall, and his shoulders looked like those of a flanker on a rugby team. Claire was fairly sure in some circumstances those shoulders could block out the sun. She was not a small-framed woman, nor had anyone ever described her as willowy. In fact, the most complimentary way to describe her figure was a true hourglass, but slightly larger on top. This guy in his rented tuxedo and cheap loafers made her feel petite and feminine.

Because of the difference in their height, Claire must have knocked into his arm, making his drink tumble out of his calloused hand and all down the front of her black and sequined halter gown. She pulled the dress away from her body.

"Here, let me help you with that," he said in a

deep baritone voice, as he stole a blatant glimpse down the front of her dress.

She let the damp gown fall back against her body where it molded to her curvaceous upper half. "I think you've done more than enough."

"Hey, it was an accident, and you bumped into me, but in my opinion, it improved the fit of your gown."

Claire looked him up and down. "As if I'd take fashion advice from you. Where did you rent that tux? Dolts Are Us?"

"If you'd like you can give it to me, and I'll have it cleaned."

"Did you seriously just ask me to take off my gown in a crowded room at a charity fundraiser?"

"I didn't mean here. You can't possibly think you're so hot, I'd jump you in front of a bunch of high-class strangers."

Maybe he hadn't meant it that way, but it didn't matter. The little girl who'd been having a wonderful time at the perfect Evangeline's graduation garden party, didn't consider the ramifications when she brought her hand back to slap him. All she could hear in that space of a heartbeat was Evangeline and her best friend, Gemma, talking about her.

"Honestly, Evangeline I don't know how you put up with the little urchin—well, I guess she's not really that little, is she?" Gemma laughed. Gemma was a bitch.

"I am beginning to believe that her grandfather must have

something on Papa." Evangeline always put the accent on the last syllable. "She is rather gauche, isn't she?"

"Gauche doesn't begin to cover it. The boarding school is going to have to order special uniforms to fit her. Maybe they'll put her on a diet. Good god, have you seen how she eats?"

Evangeline laughed her bubbling, ultra-feminine laugh that actually didn't bode well for anyone about whom she was thinking. "I swear, she's never met a pastry or carb she didn't like."

Claire looked down at her hands, which bore the telltale traces of pastry flakes from the last of the meat pasty she'd just stuffed into her mouth, as well as the grease from the contents held within. With no napkin available, she flipped up the hem of her party dress and hastily wiped her hands off on the underside.

"Are we going to have to be nice to her in Switzerland?"

"I don't know why he insisted she come to the same boarding school. I understand Papa feels some obligation to her grandfather, but honestly, couldn't he just have sent her off to Ireland? They like horses there. But Papa wouldn't listen, although he did finally give into my pleas that she not be in the same room with me. He managed to get you and I assigned to the same room."

"Party Central," trilled Gemma. "Let's hope she gets the message and stays away. She could really bring down our standing. She's fat, sloppy, and not very bright."

"Not to mention she's practically an orphan and was raised by my father's chauffeur, that no account Irishman, who spends more time with my father's horses and cars than he does poor

Claire. She'll never amount to anything. She really is a ragamuffin."

Evangeline didn't even have the good grace to seem embarrassed that Claire might have overheard them. She had. In the months and years ahead, she knew that was the moment that something hardened inside her. Something made her become determined to prove Evangeline and all her friends wrong. And she had.

They admired her now for her outer worldly success. She was seen as one of the most successful art recovery and restoration experts in the world. Her Tudor-era studio and home were located in an old millhouse in Greenwich on the River Thames, just outside London. The renovation and her business had been covered and photographed in numerous art, home, and architectural magazines. Her services were in demand with some of the biggest and wealthiest insurance companies and individuals in the world.

Claire had watched and learned. She looked and dressed like them. She still might not fit into those designer clothes, but she could afford to have close copies made that fit her within an inch of her life.

She snapped out of her reverie when the man in front of her caught her wrist.

"That's enough," he said with an edge to his voice that indicated he was used to people following his commands. "It was an accident, and I've offered to have your dress cleaned. Besides which, the day I decide to have my way with you, I won't ask for the damn dress, I'll take it."

"Claire, don't." Mia said stridently in her ear. "Whatever it is you're thinking don't. People are starting to look your way. Get out of there. They're flashing the lights. The event is winding down and they're going to take the necklace. You don't have much time to get into position. Ask yourself which is more important? Ripping this guy's nuts off and shoving him down his throat, or getting the Grenadine Necklace back to its rightful owner."

She stepped back and tugged her arm from his grasp. "Of course, you're right. My apologies for letting my temper get the best of me. It's been a long evening." She turned to walk away.

Mr. Muscle in his Dolts Are Us tuxedo and cheap shoes, moved with speed and grace and put himself in her way once again. If he made her miss this chance at the necklace, she was going to do some damage to this asshole.

"Don't let it concern you. I did spill my drink down your dress. I would like a chance to make it up to you. Why don't you come to the Savoy tomorrow and bring your dress? I'll have it cleaned while we have breakfast. They have the most amazing staff there. I'm convinced that there isn't anything the head concierge, Felix, can't do. He's pretty amazing."

"Is that really how you'd prefer we meet for breakfast?"

"Claire, stop it," Mia hissed in her ear.

"No, what I'd prefer is for you to roll over and we order from room service, but I was worried if I told you that, you might give into the impulse you had to do something very unladylike to my nuts, which I'm very fond of."

Claire stepped back, shaking her head. "No. I think I will avoid the Savoy until you leave."

She needed to put distance between them. This was not the kind of man to whom she allowed herself to be attracted. She preferred the more leanly muscled men of London's elite—those who made their money, and lots of it, with their minds and not their broad shoulders, devastating smiles, and calloused hands. But if she was being honest with herself, she'd never been more wildly attracted to any man in her life. She could well imagine those rough hands skimming over her body and grasping her hips as he plunged into her again and again.

No. Not going there. That way lies heartache and madness!

He took a step toward her. "How will you know? You don't even know my name."

"Nor do I want to." The lights flickered again. "They're signaling for us to leave—make sure you take your cheap shoes with you. They'll never pass for glass slippers, and I really don't want to see how bad all of this," she said circling her finger to indicate all of him, "gets at the stroke of midnight."

Claire hurried away from him, ensuring he wasn't

following her. People were already leaving the building as she made her way toward the woman's loo. Once inside, she locked the door, kicked off her heels and searched for the air duct that would be sealed the following day.

Standing on the toilet in the last stall, she pried the grate off the ducting. "Okay, Mia, I'm in place. Tell me when to activate and send the canister." There was no snarky comeback. There was silence on the other end. "Mia? Mia, this is not funny. I get it; you hate it when I go dark on you. I won't do it again." Still nothing. "Mia?"

"Fuck," said Claire, putting the canister back in her clutch.

For Mia to not answer, something had to have gone very wrong. Claire needed to get out without anyone taking notice of her, and she needed to get to Mia.

Unlocking the door to the loo, she joined a small crowd of stragglers and exited the venue. Claire walked to the end of the block, uncertain as to whether to go to the point where Mia had dropped her off or the one where they planned to rendezvous. Chances were Mia had not remained at the drop point and Claire had been talking to her right up until she was supposed to give her the go ahead to get the necklace.

Fearful Mia had been pinched, discovered, or worse, Claire raced to the agreed upon meeting place, praying that her need to make things right had not harmed Mia. It took every fiber of self-control that she had not to race down the street calling for her friend. She was vaguely aware that the Grenadine Necklace might now be lost to her, but that was a poor consideration next to Mia's safety. Claire could not allow herself to even contemplate losing Mia.

CHAPTER 3

CLAIRE

*O*nce she had left the street and entered the dark alleys, Claire removed her high heels and ran as fast as her feet would carry her, watching for anything that might cut her feet. There was a small semblance of relief when she saw the van right where it was supposed to be. The lights were off and there was no smoke coming out of the tailpipe, but Mia often turned the van off and relied on generators to run all of her tech gear. She said if the van was parked and the motor and lights were left on, it tended to look suspicious.

Reason returned to the fore and Claire slowed down, looking around for something to use as a weapon. The canister of the knock-out gas would be no good, as she would dose herself if she wasn't careful. No rebar, no hunks of wood with nails in them, just your normal London garbage. Maybe it was time to rethink carrying a gun or some kind of mace.

Claire slinked along the side of the van between it and the wall of the building it was parked next to. When she finally reached the passenger side door's window, she peaked in. Mia had her head down, furiously punching her keyboard. Claire tapped on the side panel door and breathed a sigh of relief as she stepped inside.

Closing the door behind her, she hit the automatic lock. "What the hell, Mia?"

"We've got problems."

"I gathered that when the comms unit went dead."

Mia looked up and smiled. "You were worried about me."

"Of course, I was worried about you. You're my best friend."

"I'm your only friend."

"Even more reason for me to be concerned."

"From what I overheard, the guy who spilled the drink down your dress wouldn't have minded signing on."

"Oh, please. He had on some cheap, rented tux, his shoes looked like he'd thrown them in the wash to get them clean, his hair was a mess, he had at least a day's growth of beard, and he works with his hands."

"Good with his hands is never a bad thing."

Mia scrabbled past Claire to get into the driver's

seat, start the engine and pull away. "You weren't followed, were you?" Her eyes checked the rear and side view mirrors.

Claire joined her up front. "Of course not. What happened? I was in place."

"I know. I was watching the men remove the necklace and they were moving toward the deserted exhibition hall. I was waiting to get everything in place and then nothing. I couldn't hear you; my ability to use their cameras to see you vanished. Like in the blink of an eye. Nothing. I tried to reach you over the comm. I even tried your cell phone. There was nothing. It was as if someone had dropped a shroud over the van. I was completely and utterly jammed."

"Who could do that?"

"Not many people outside the government. I mean, there are one or two black ops groups. Only Cerberus is based here in London, but then there's also the alphabet agencies—some homegrown and some from around the world. You've pissed off a lot of people, Claire. People we shouldn't have been messing with."

"I may have gone after them personally, but I never took anything from any government. They're taking the necklace back to Paris. Do we know how? Any chance we can snatch it before then? I know how you feel about *Chateau des Templiers*. Maybe there's an opportunity…"

"I think you may have to give this one up. That's twice we've tried, and twice we've missed…"

"You know what they say, third time's the charm."

"We got to kind of skate by tonight, but the last time you almost got caught. I think we need to go dark for a while. The fact that someone has made a run at us digitally…"

"But they've failed."

"That's not really the point. The fact is, they know we're here. These have been targeted attacks, and tonight they jammed me completely, which means either they knew where we were physically, or they know enough about us digitally that they could do it. I'm not really sure which worries me more."

Claire reached out and squeezed Mia's arm. "I'm sorry. I get so focused on winning the prize that sometimes I forget the toll it takes on you. If you think we should step back, we'll step back."

Mia shook her head. "Don't do that. You are not responsible for any of what happened tonight. We've had a good run without any issues. I've always known at some point, someone was going to start trying to link things together and figure out if there was a pattern and if so, who was responsible. I think they are a long way from knowing who we are. They've just figured out there is someone. I just need some time to build a digital maze with several catastrophic ends for them and construct some new fire walls."

"I don't know what I'd do without you."

"You'd have been caught a long time ago," Mia laughed. "I know your granda was the best when he was young, but back in his day, they didn't have to go up against all the electronic and digital alarms, sentries, and other devices."

"I'm going to follow your lead on this one. The last thing we need is for anyone to figure out what we're up to and who we might be. We'll get our shot, or maybe it just wasn't meant to be."

Mia nodded as she drove to the warehouse where they kept the van. From there, Claire would take Mia home to Chelsea before heading to her own home and bed in Greenwich.

FLETCH

Curious girl—bold, beautiful, and bodacious. Not like so many of the women—men, too—at these kinds of events. They tended to make polite small talk while trying to figure out who they should be seen with. Instead, she'd insulted his tuxedo and his shoes, but the pupils of her eyes had flared briefly when he suggested what he'd been thinking. He didn't think she was the usual rich girl looking for a little rough and dirty with the lower class. She'd been right about what he was wearing, but Ryland Fletcher would have bet money on the fact that she had not been 'to the manor born.'

Fletch was impressed by her willingness to speak her mind and show her emotions, but she'd fled before he could truly engage with her. When he'd caught a glimpse of her again, he'd thought of giving chase, but he'd needed to ensure the necklace got into the hands of the courier. The armed guard and the armored car had been a ruse.

Give chase. Now there was an intriguing thought.

When she'd re-emerged from the back of the venue, he'd thought to catch up with her and maybe take her for a drink or a late supper. That was what he would have proposed. What he really wanted was to take her back to his hotel and spend the rest of the night enjoying all the pleasure her body and temperament had promised. He moved toward her, but she was quickly swallowed up by the crowd.

"Mr. Fletcher," said the very honorable Edgar Pennington, the museum's director. "I take it the necklace is back in safe hands?"

"As safe as we can make it," he said extending his hand and shaking Pennington's. "I appreciate your cooperation and assistance. Our man has the necklace and it is being transported to an airport north of here." Fletch glanced at his watch. "He should be airborne within the hour."

"I was surprised to see Lloyds and the other insurance carrier so keen to hire you to protect it."

"There were some rumors that an attempt had been made previously. Nobody wants to see that thing stolen."

"Wouldn't it be hard to sell?"

"Not necessarily. There are those who like to acquire famous, or preferably infamous, pieces of jewelry just to enjoy for themselves. As I said, we believe there was a previous attempt, so we just wanted to be extra cautious."

"Is there anything specific about the Grenadine Necklace that would make it a target?"

"It depends on who you ask. The necklace itself is an exquisite representation of art deco jewelry making, and the gems are close to flawless. Where it gets tricky—and what attracts some less than ethical buyers—is that it is heavily rumored to have been stolen by or for Mussolini, who gave it to his mistress. The current owner has provenance, but over the years there have been some questions as to its authenticity. Thank you, again."

"It was my pleasure. I appreciate you pointing out some cracks in our security arsenal. It was most beneficial."

"My pleasure." Fletch glanced at his watch. "I'm sorry. I need to check in with my people."

None of his people were in London—only one other member of the team was here. Fletch really didn't have to check in with anyone, but he'd had his fill of officious people for the day. Pennington was all right in that old money, stick-up-his-butt kind of way, but he grated on Fletch. He wondered if the curvy brunette would have joined him for a burger and a brew. Good burgers were hard to find in London, but he knew all the best places.

Fletch had a sudden vision of the woman who had eluded him naked in the middle of his bed, eating a juicy cheeseburger and dipping her fries in ketchup. No, not ketchup. That was far too mundane. Ranch dressing? Blue Cheese? Sriracha?

As he made his way out of the building, his phone chimed. He glanced at the text. The package was airborne. He quickly texted his counterpart in Paris. That meant he was officially done for the day—technically yesterday, as it was a little past midnight.

He hailed a cab and made his way back to the Savoy. There were glitzier, flashier, more expensive hotels in London, but to Fletch, none compared to the Savoy. It was the only place he would stay when he was in the English capital.

"Mr. Fletcher," said the concierge as he entered the building.

Fletch smiled but continued to his room without reply. Opening the door to his suite, he flipped on the light and got a look at himself in the mirror. She was right. The tuxedo didn't fit well and looked cheap. If he continued to take these high-end security jobs, perhaps he ought to invest in a custom tuxedo.

He tossed the jacket and tie onto the chair, unbuttoning his shirt as he made himself comfortable on the settee. 'Settee,' he snorted.

We call them loveseats back in the States.

He turned on the television, searching for a twenty-four-hour news channel. Finding one, he opened his phone and pulled up the guest list from the party. He might not know her name, but with each ticket sold, he had a picture and dossier downloaded. He scrolled through the list until he found her—Claire Mitchell.

The photo was excellent. There was no doubt she was the woman he'd spilled the drink on, but other than that, the dossier seemed a bit sparse. She was an art restorer with an excellent reputation. There was a lot of information regarding her work, but little seemed to be known about her private life other than she had restored an old millhouse on the River Thames outside of London. It contained her private studio in the lower portion with the open concept living space being on the second level including a powder room and chef's kitchen and two bedrooms, each with an attached bath on the third. The water wheel worked and supplied most of her energy needs.

Her ticket had been given to her as a thank you for a sizeable donation, but the RSVP and the ticket itself had not been entered until only a couple of hours before she ran into him—literally. Something about her had set off warning bells and red flags, and he'd planned to get a better look at her to figure out if she was someone he needed to be concerned about.

When she'd run into him, it felt like the perfect opportunity to spill his drink on her to check for any bugs, tracking equipment, or other electronic devices. There hadn't been any he could see. He supposed he could have used the scanner in his pocket but dousing her with gin and tonic had the added benefit of revealing the gorgeous body that lay beneath her rather conservative gown. How he would have loved to unzip that dress so he could slip his hand inside and caress her ass.

Claire Mitchell had a lovely ass and a voluptuous body. She was, as they used to say in his unit, fine as fuck with dangerous curves. What was that old *Bon Jovi* album… *'Slippery When Wet?'* He was pretty damn sure he could get her wet enough that he'd slide right in and ride her hard enough to create the kind of friction that would make her scream his name and cling to him.

His cock throbbed with need. Fletch knew if he went down to the American Bar just off the lobby at the Savoy he could find an engaging companion for the night, but that no longer interested him. What had caught his attention was Claire Mitchell and her less than forthright dossier.

Fletch spent the next several hours running down information about the curvaceous woman with the long dark hair. By the time he was finished, he had a whole lot of nothing. Plenty about her business and skills as an art appraiser and restorer, as well as the house she had brought back from the edge of condemnation. The space was beautiful, but not as ornate as he might have thought, and her workspace had a kind of messy inviting quality.

He sat back and looked at the data he had collected.

Who are you, Claire Mitchell? And why do you call to me the way you do?

CHAPTER 4

CLAIRE

*S*unlight filtered in through the gossamer sheers that hung from the windows on either side of her bedroom. There was no need for anything that offered more privacy as one window looked out onto the River Thames and the other onto the old mill wheel. Some people found solace in the waves of the ocean. Claire found it in the steadily turning water wheel as it splashed through the water, scooping it up only to let it fall with a pattering sound like a heavy rain from a gutter as it completed its rhythmic circle.

Mia would be here soon. They wanted to go over their plans for their next heist outside of London. Claire knew she should get out of bed and get dressed. Unlike many people, Claire preferred to shower at night. Her property had a small barn and she continued to keep horses, ride, and compete in equestrian events. She rode most evenings and so preferred to shower afterwards so she didn't go to bed early smelling of horses. Even when she didn't ride, she most often showered right before bed.

Drawing her legs up, Claire hugged them to her chest and smiled as she laid her head on her knees. Poppi. He'd been gone for more than a decade, but she never failed to think of horses without thinking of him.

Her first clear-cut memory—one that she could see in her mind's eye—was of being atop a caramel-colored pony with a blonde mane and tail. Poppi was leading her under a canopy of weeping willows at the top of the hill, which rolled gently down to a pond that was home to several pairs of Mute Swans.

Ducking under the graceful bows as they walked in and out of the dappled sunlight, Claire knew there had to have been other people around, but her memory was based on a child's interpretation and remembrance of the unconditional love that Poppi had bestowed on her.

"Are ya havin' fun, darlin'?" he asked her as he strode along, the placid pony following just behind and to the side of him.

"Yes, Poppi," she answered, lifting her face to the sky and stretching her arms wide to embrace the entire universe, truly believing the world was her oyster and that she would only find priceless pearls within.

"That's me girl."

She might have lost her parents in a horrific accident as an infant, and as a teenager she'd had to face some brutal truths, but the in-between had been truly idyllic. She glanced at the clock on the mantle of the fireplace.

One thing about the Tudors—they crafted beautiful fireplaces. The one downstairs in her studio was an ornate masterpiece. It had taken her months to restore it. Both fireplaces worked, but she had kept them more for their beauty and master craftsmanship than for their functionality. She had a sophisticated and hidden HVAC system to keep the house warm and cozy in the winter and cool and comfortable in the summer.

Her mind drifted back to the night before. Instead of focusing on the target and how they might have done things differently, all she could think of was the hunky guy who'd spilled his drink all down the front of her dress.

Did he really say to me that if he decided to have me, he wouldn't ask for my dress? The implication being he would rip it from her. Why was it the thought of that lit up her whole erotic system? She had no doubt he could do it, probably had done it, but the idea that he would want to do it with her made her nipples pebble and her pussy clench. Men like him didn't make suggestions like that to 'curvy girls' like her.

"He isn't here; so, get your arse out of bed, girl," the little voice inside her head whispered. Her little voice was blunt to the point of rudeness, but it did have a point.

He wasn't here, the horses needed to be fed and Mia would be here at any time.

Claire knew that Mia had always been in favor of her changing up her look and either renting an Airbnb or a hotel room when she was casing a place. While it might prove necessary when looking at private estates, to Claire it made perfect sense to go into museums as herself to have a look around. After all, she and Poppi hadn't spent all that money for her to get an art degree if she wasn't going to use it.

"I don't want to go, Poppi. I can learn so much from you. I don't want to work in a stuffy old museum."

"And I don't want to see you end up in prison. I don't want you in this life."

What he didn't know was that she had a plan—a plan to continue on with his mission to restore the things he'd stolen to their rightful owners.

In the end, she had done as Poppi wanted and graduated with a doctorate in conservation from the Fine Arts Institute of Monaco, and a commission from the ruling family there had set her reputation. Nonetheless, she would not be swayed from her plan. It wasn't until Poppi caught her boosting something from his cache that he'd confronted her for a second time.

"Did ya think I wouldn't notice there were pieces missing?"

"I guess I didn't care. I'm only trying to follow in your footsteps—trying to make things right. There are people to whom

these things rightfully belong. They aren't the ones I stole them from."

"I'm well aware of that'," he said with a tolerant tone and a smile tugging at the corners of his mouth.

"Don't you trot out your Irish charm. It doesn't work on me and hasn't since I was twelve. I guess I don't understand why you've risked everything for people you never even knew. I could understand if you took them to sell so that you could afford to take care of me and give me all the things you thought I needed, but how did you choose the people to steal from? Some of them are our friends."

Poppi smiled. "As I said, you don't understand. Let's go sit at the kitchen table. You can make your old granda a proper cup of tea."

He walked past her, taking her hand and leading her into the small kitchen in the carriage house where she'd grown up.

"First those people you set such store by? The ones you think are our friends? Their children might be your friends, but their parents look down on me and you both."

She remembered the conversation she'd overheard between Evangeline and Gemma.

"Maybe, but it's still too close to home. I recognized Lady Haversham's brooch, and I heard the maids whispering about it being stolen."

"Aye. I took the brooch. But it was never Lady Haversham's. It was part of a cache of jewels taken out of one of the Nazi concentration camps. Sir Godfrey's father and some of his old chums used World War II as their own investment scheme. That brooch once belonged to a French family by the name of

Geller. They lost everything. Only one son survived because he wasn't there when the Gestapo came calling."

"Do you think Lady Haversham knows?" she asked, fascinated.

"Doubtful. But her da and Sir Godfrey's were up to their neck in looted Nazi treasure. I took the brooch and mean to see it gets back to its rightful owner. He's an old man now, but it will mean something to his children, and their children."

"So, if you're not stealing the jewels and selling them, then how do we afford everything?"

"I found out what Sir Godfrey's da had done. The old bastard tried to kill me. He missed and your parents paid the price…"

"Sir Godfrey's father killed my parents? Why didn't you have them arrested?" she asked as she steeped the tea before pouring him a mug.

"What good would it do? The old man was dying. Besides, it wasn't going to bring your parents back, and I had my grand-daughter to raise. So, I made a deal with the old man and Sir Godfrey. In exchange for my silence, I would be allowed to live and work here on the estate. I would be paid a good wage, would get to live here rent free, and you would be afforded every privilege Sir Godfrey's own daughter was. After a while that seemed selfish and unfair to those they had robbed; so, I started stealing from those with the ill-gotten goods and returning them to where they belonged."

"No one ever guessed?"

Poppi shrugged. "Godfrey may have guessed, but he couldn't prove anything, and he was more concerned with preserving the family name than getting rid of me or getting his friends' things back to them."

Pouring a mug of her own, she sat down in the chair next to him and put her free hand over his. "You're too old for this kind of thing, Poppi. Teach me and let me carry on your legacy."

They had argued the rest of the night, but in the end, Claire had made him see sense, and made him understand that his legacy living on was important enough to allow Claire to risk herself... and so she had.

Outside, a car door slammed right before the bell over the entry into her studio jingled.

"Claire? It's me! I'm coming up."

Claire shook her head. Who the hell else would it be? After all, Mia was the only one with a key and the security code.

"Come on up. I'll brew us some tea," Claire said, exiting her bedroom and stretching—her midriff showing between the roomy boy shorts and the ribbed tank top.

Mia smiled. "Whenever I see you all dolled up, I wonder if those boys drooling all over themselves have any idea what a slob you are at heart. If my mother had ever seen you dressed like that, she'd have had a case of the vapors."

Claire rolled her eyes. "It's a well-documented fact that the 'vapors' were caused by women having their corsets cinched too tight. They literally couldn't breathe."

"You just made that up," Mia accused.

"Did I?" Claire teased.

"You're terrible. I don't know why I put up with being your friend."

"Because if it wasn't for me and my Triumph Spitfire, you'd be married to Reginald Walker."

"God, wouldn't that have just been awful?"

Claire had grumbled all the way to the beautiful gothic cathedral in the north. Poppi had insisted that she go, reminding her that Mia was her best friend and that regardless of what Claire thought of her fiancé, Claire should be there to support her. Claire had argued that it would be disingenuous at best.

They had finally agreed to a compromise—Claire would take a wedding gift to Mia and wish her nothing but happiness in her future. So now she was driving her restored vintage Triumph Spitfire up to York to deliver something Poppi had picked out from one of the bridal registries Mia had signed up for.

The cathedral's parking lot was filled to the brim, and valets were parking people's cars in the field next door. If it rained, that was going to be a huge mess. Instead, Claire parked in the small alley between the cathedral and one of its adminis-trative buildings. She was only going to be there for a few minutes.

As soon as she arrived, Mia shooed everyone out, saying she wanted a few minutes alone with Claire. Everyone who knew she and Mia had made mention of the fact that Claire had been absent not only from the wedding party but from every pre-wedding activity.

Claire walked into the room and Mia spun around, closing the door so she could lock and lean against it.

"Mia? Are you okay?"

Mia said nothing.

"Mia?"

Nothing.

"Mia? Just tell me you love him."

Nothing.

"Shit, Mia. Are you standing there in that god awful wedding dress I'm sure your mother picked out and telling me you are not in love with that prick, but you're going to go through with this farce?"

"Wha… What are we going to do?"

"What do you mean we? How the hell did you let this happen?"

"I don't know. Everybody kept pushing him at me and telling me what a great catch he was and how we'd make the perfect couple. So, I just went along with everything, and it kind of snowballed."

"'Kind of snowballed?' There are hundreds of people down there."

"I know," Mia said on the verge of panicking. "So, what are we going to do?"

Claire ran over to the window and looked down. Turning to Mia, she said, "First thing we do is get you out of that monstrosity. Please tell me you have real clothes." Mia nodded. "Good. We need you to get redressed."

"This gown is a pain in the arse to get in and out of. What are we doing?"

Claire glanced around smiling as she saw a pair of scissors. "We're going to pull a Thelma and Louise on them—only skipping the part where we kill Brad Pitt and then drive my car off a cliff."

Between the two of them, using their hands and scissors, they had Mia out of the dress in no time. Once she was in leggings, a sweater and a pair of sneakers, they eased out the bride's room window, made their way down the fire escape and hopped into Claire's car.

Claire fired the engine, put it in gear, and floored it.

"Mia! Mia!" called Reginald who had only just arrived for the ceremony.

"Stop the car," said Mia, shocking Claire who did as her friend asked. Mia jumped out of the car, twisting her engagement ring off her finger and shoving it into Reginald's hand. "Marry Lizzie. You two love each other. We'd have made each other miserable. Have a great life!"

Mia had run back to the car with her family in hot pursuit. The second she was in, Claire gunned the engine and tore out of the parking lot, spewing dirt and gravel everywhere.

"I guess you really saved my arse that time," agreed Mia.

Claire reached over and took her hands. "And we've been saving each other's ever since."

"Remember how we were lamenting about not being able to get the necklace?" Claire nodded. "It seems the plane they were taking had to turn back because of engine trouble. The insurance companies want it back at the museum. That case and everything around it was designed to keep it safe."

"Do you think we can get a second shot at it?"

"Didn't you tell me the third time's the charm? Besides, I'll call in a favor from Lizzie. She's some kind of tech guru these days. She always said she owed me. Did you know they named their first daughter Mia Claire? The necklace should be there for at least two weeks."

"That means we have until then to figure out *if* they jammed our communications and shut us down and *how.*"

"I'm going to get Lizzie to help me look at some of the code I discovered that isn't mine. Maybe she can figure out how it got there and how to make it inert. I don't want them to know we discovered it; I just want to render it useless. I'm also going to have her look at some of my hardware. It's top of the line, but you never know."

For the rest of the day, they plotted and schemed, coming up with and discarding several plans until they weeded them out to a primary plan and a backup. Claire was certain she could come up with a reason to spend some time in the museum. Pennington was a pompous ass, but he could be a useful tool. While she was there, she'd see what other weaknesses or security systems they might have put into place.

"I should be able to spend some time in there."

"I'm almost done programming those new glasses. If you can wear those and at least get one good visual, the hidden camera will record everything, and we can spend some time comparing what we get to what's on the blueprints."

"So much for shop talk. It's time for chocolate chip mint ice cream with Bailey's."

Mia grinned. It was her absolute favorite.

With their preliminary plans set for taking another stab at snatching the Grenadine Necklace, Claire saw Mia out to her car, waving to her in the twilight before checking a final time on her horses. Something about the sound of horses munching hay seemed to put things right with the world.

Claire stripped out of her clothes and took a quick shower before crawling between the sheets without putting anything on. Sleeping naked always gave her a feeling of control and freedom from societal norms she enjoyed. It was only when Mia, who was notoriously early, was coming that she bothered with anything at all.

There was something far more exhausting about planning a heist than riding and caring for her horses. As she tried to get comfortable and settle down in bed, she realized it wasn't Poppi, her horses, or even those for whom she risked so much, it was the dark-haired man with the fathomless eyes and hard-muscled body who occupied her thoughts.

She'd chided him for his rumpled, rented tuxedo and his calloused hands, but the thought of those same strong, roughhewn hands running over her naked body while he whispered all the delightfully dirty things he was going to do to her was something she could well imagine and longed to experience. It was easy to imagine his thumbs strumming and plucking at her nipples while he cupped her breasts in his hands.

Claire stretched out in bed, allowing her hand to slide down her body to reach between her legs to tickle her clit and play with her pussy. She began to rub her swollen nub, looking for some relief from the pent-up stress as she pinched her own nipples. It would be easier if she used her vibrator, but she didn't want to stop.

Normally, she just focused on the pleasure she was giving herself, but tonight she was distracted by all she had to do and the fact that twice she had failed to achieve her goal. Claire didn't like losing and didn't have much practice at it. She closed her eyes and the man in the bad tuxedo stood before her. Only this time he didn't have on a tuxedo. In fact, he didn't have on anything at all.

She could well imagine how all of those muscles resulting in broad shoulders, sculpted pecs, and washboard abs went with his handsome face and big dick. He had to have a big dick, right? Big, hard, and fully engorged—it would take a licking and keep on ticking.

Yeah, that was the ticket. She could feel her body starting to ramp up as she pinched her nipples tighter and rubbed her clit, imagining that it was him.

"Next time, sweetheart. Next time," he crooned to her as her orgasm crashed down all around her and she cried out, allowing the intense pleasure to suffuse her system.

Sitting up in bed, she realized the night was lost to finding sleep. Sleep would come when she had obtained her prize. The question now was which prize she wanted more—the necklace or the man?

CHAPTER 5

C *laire*
  To some, the idea of taking the underground into London on a lovely, sunny day would seem incongruous. But to Claire, it was an easy, quick way into the city and meant she didn't have to worry about a vehicle. There were so many ways to travel from Greenwich to London—train, underground, boat—that not having to worry about a vehicle made the decision easy. She supposed for most, the underground would have been the least likely choice, but for Claire, the darkness seemed more anonymous, and exiting with a crowd of people meant the CCTV would have more trouble spotting her.

  Claire had opted for a crinkled bohemian skirt, a belted sweater that fell past her ass, and her riding boots. She'd thought about using the headband to

obscure her face, but Mia was right—it did kind of
look like a tiara. Besides, it would be harder to explain
why she didn't show up on the museum's video
footage when she was meeting with Pennington, the
director of the museum. She would be wearing her
'fancy' glasses but figured with her hair up in a messy
bun they fit the art restorer/nerdy vibe. She also
figured she'd be able to fit into her surroundings
better.

She had to get her head into the game. Sleep last
night had been elusive at best. The past few nights,
the man in the rumpled tuxedo had invaded her
thoughts and dreams. Trying to focus on the job at
hand was proving to be more difficult than it had ever
been. Who was he? The reality was, she'd probably
never know, and she reminded herself, that was as it
should be. She didn't have time for a relationship. Did
that exclude having an intense sexual interlude with
him for a weekend? Not necessarily.

The underground train pulled into the station and
Claire exited with the other commuters and headed
up the steps onto London's busy streets. It was a short
walk to Mia's home, where she was already getting set
up for their surveillance and video of the venue and
the necklace's location.

Mia answered the knock on her door, hustling her
inside.

"Problem?" Claire asked.

"Not necessarily, but I did reach out to Lizzie, and she was able to track the cyber hits and jamming we encountered back to a high-end security group: Silver Arrow Security. She couldn't get past their firewalls, and neither can I. To tell the truth, this group is really off the general public's radar. Where Cerberus is written about all the time, very few people know about Silver Arrow. I can't even find any kind of corporate information listing the owner or owners. All very hush-hush."

"Why would they be looking at us?"

"Conjecture only, but maybe the current owner or the current owner's insurance agency brought them in after our first attempt."

"How good are they?" asked Claire.

"I asked Lizzie the same question, only I asked how dangerous this level of subterfuge and camouflage made them, and she said: 'very.' So we need to be careful and you need to ask yourself if it's worth taking you out. I know you don't care nearly as much about your personal safety as you do mine, but if something happens to you, who's going to play Robin Hood for the rest of these people?"

"I know you're right; I do. I just hate being beaten. I tell you what, how about this is our last shot at the Grenadine Necklace? If I can't snatch it this time, we'll consider it gone. And from now on, if we can't get it the first time, we walk away."

"And after tomorrow, we lay low for a few months?"

"Deal. Maybe we'll take some time and go check out the cabana boys in Aruba for a month—maybe take a cruise back to the UK."

"Can we have some of those drinks with the little umbrellas in them? I've always wanted one of those."

"Done," Claire said, smiling at how Mia's whole body seemed to relax—the tension gone from her body and her eyes softening. "Do you have my glasses ready?"

Mia nodded. "I do, indeed. Why this particular pair?"

"Because I wanted them to go with my outfit and they fit the whole Claire Mitchell, Art Restorer vibe. I need to look like I belong at these museums, galleries, and charity events. My granda used to always say 'hide in plain sight.'"

Within minutes, Claire was headed out of Mia's house and to the Met. She entered the bright, shiny, modern building, which she knew had been inspired by the Louvre's pyramid. It seemed incongruous that a building of light and glass housed incredible exhibits of the old-world Masters.

Stopping at the reception desk, she asked for Edgar Pennington.

The woman looked her up and down and all but wrinkled her nose at Claire's bohemian style. "I'm sorry, but the director doesn't see anyone without an appointment."

"I have an appointment," Claire said. "In fact, Mr. Pennington is the one who made it. I'm Claire Mitchell. If he's changed his mind…"

"Dr. Mitchell, I'm so sorry. I didn't recognize you. Yes, you are on the director's schedule, but I also know you are one of the few people who wouldn't need to be. He would clear everything off his schedule in order to meet with you. If you'll just follow me…"

"I'd prefer to wait here. He wanted me to look at a couple of paintings and I am pressed for time so the sooner I can talk to him about specifics, the better."

"Of course, I understand. Just wait here—better yet, take one of these, and then you can wander to your heart's content. It will let us know where to find you."

Claire smiled and adjusted her glasses as she took the little device that resembled an old-school pager. "That would be great."

"Keep it away from your glasses," whispered Mia in her ear. "It could jam the video signal."

Claire watched as the woman from reception scurried away. She wasn't sure if the woman was afraid of Pennington or just flabbergasted to be in her presence. The latter was just plain silly. Claire was good at her job, but Poppi had taught her that people should expect the best from you. Taking her tracking device, she wandered into one of the light-filled galleries. She glanced up at the windows, seeing the sunny blue skies with tufts of white, cotton candy clouds and wondering if the purity of sunlight that poured through the glass ceiling didn't damage the paint on the works of art. She was also looking to see if there was a better way of ingress or egress.

"There are filament fibers inserted in the glass that filter out the harmful rays," whispered the sexy voice from the fundraising gala the other night.

That he had slipped in so close to her was disconcerting. She had honed her senses to where it was difficult, if not impossible, for someone to sneak up on her. The fact that he had done so to the point where she could feel his breath on the back of her neck was worrisome, as well as incredibly erotic. For such a large, brawny man he moved with the grace and elegance of a large, predatory cat.

Claire whirled around. She was here to get the necklace, not to get laid. She needed to back him off and back him off now. "Do you always sneak up on women like that?"

She couldn't help but notice the incongruousness of the tailored wool trousers, high end cotton shirt and polished shoes with the shlumpy tuxedo he'd worn to the gala.

"Only the ones I want to seduce," he said with a feral grin.

Did he just say he wants to seduce me?

Shaking her head, she tapped the edge of her glasses. "Never happen."

"Hmm; we'll see."

"Arrogant bastard," she hissed. "Go away."

"Ahh, Dr. Mitchell," said Edgar Pennington as he approached them. "I see that you have met Mr. Fletcher."

"Fletcher?" she asked.

"Yes," he said with an easy smile. "Ryland Fletcher, and you're Dr. Claire Mitchell, the famous restoration specialist."

So did he know her by reputation, or had he done some digging on his own? Time to give him something to think about.

"Ryland Fletcher of Silver Arrow Security. That's kind of cute, by the way—Fletcher as in a man who makes arrows."

Fletcher nodded.

"Good. I'm glad you two have met. Mr. Fletcher was very helpful in pointing out some flaws in our security system."

Well, that settled it; Fletcher had to have been the one who, at the very least jammed their comm units the night of the gala, and in all likelihood had been attacking the firewalls of Mia's system. Yet another reason she needed to avoid Ryland Fletcher.

"Mr. Pennington?" she said, spinning smoothly on

the ball of her foot so that her back was once again to Fletcher. "You asked me to meet you today to show me a couple of paintings... you needed my professional opinion on their appraised value, their provenance, and whether they needed restoration. Would you like to show me which paintings in particular you are thinking of?"

"Yes. Of particular interest is a painting by John Atkinson Grimshaw," he said, leading the way into another gallery, where he stopped in front of a painting Claire knew all too well.

It was one of Grimshaw's lesser-known works, a still life, but there was no doubt as to its authenticity. Poppi had been looking for this piece for decades.

"He is considered the father and master of moonlit landscapes known as 'nocturnes,'" she started, "but he did do other subjects—fairies and still lifes in particular."

"You know your English painters," chimed in Fletcher, who had not taken a hint when she turned her back on him and had followed her and Mr. Pennington.

"I do have a doctorate, Mr. Fletcher. I would think you would assume I knew fine art. I will tell you that I'd love to get a look at the provenance on this painting. It disappeared during the second world war. Many experts considered it lost to the Nazis and the other disreputable men who looted the concentration camps and stole from those who couldn't fight back."

Pennington looked as though someone had just stolen his favorite marble. "The owner assured me…"

"I'm able to authenticate the piece itself and its appraised value, but I should let you know that I will also send a copy of my findings to the German Limbach Commission."

Pennington blanched as Claire continued, "I'm not sure your client will thank you for calling me in. Of course, you can choose to hire someone other than me whose ethics are spongier than my own."

The Limbach Commission had been charged with restoring artwork confiscated by the Nazis. The Commission had done little in the way of helping those from whom priceless artifacts were stolen. They did an excellent job of categorizing and listing pieces that had been stolen, but once they resurfaced in a museum's collection or at an auction, the Commission seemed to lose its ability or willingness to step in and spearhead the years and years of legal battles for one of the victims to have their stolen property returned to them.

Pennington showed her two more pieces, which Claire suspected had come from the same collector. All three were, as far as she knew, among the hundred thousand or more pieces of artwork that the Nazis had stolen but had yet to be recovered. Each time she moved in to take a closer look, she activated the camera.

In the van Mia was running real-time comparisons to pictures of the originals. "Holy shit," Mia whispered. "All three are on the Commission's list."

"Mr. Pennington, are you aware that all three of these paintings have been listed with the Limbach Commission as having questionable provenance?"

"The individual loaning the museum these pieces assures me the provenance is in order and that there is no question as to the legality of their ownership."

Claire looked through her phone to find the files in question and showed them to Pennington. "I suggest your buyer is either uninformed or a liar. But in any case, I am going to let the Commission know I saw all three pieces. I suspect you and your buyer will hear from them and the legitimate owner within short order. For the record, while I could appraise and restore your client's pieces, I won't. I don't deal in blood antiquities."

"But you came here today to talk to me about the work," Pennington said.

"True, but I had no way of knowing the pieces were stolen or even had questionable provenance. You failed to disclose that to me."

"I didn't know…"

"I'm sorry, but you should have."

Pennington bustled off, and Claire turned toward the gallery where the necklace had gone back to being on display. Her line of sight was completely blocked by the wall of man chest in front of her.

"Ethical and beautiful," Fletcher said softly.

"Is there something I can help you with Mr. Fletcher?"

Taking her hand, he tucked it into the crook of his arm. "Why don't you show me around the museum?"

Claire removed her hand. "This isn't my museum. There are plenty of docents who would be happy to show you around."

Fletcher recaptured her hand and put it back in the crook of his arm. "But I prefer your company."

"Why?"

"Why not? You are beautiful, intelligent, and intriguing."

Intriguing? What the hell does he mean by that? Has he reviewed the camera footage?

"I was surprised when I saw you on the guest list. I didn't realize when I bumped into you just who you were," he said smoothly. "I really wish you would let me pay for cleaning your gown, and if it's ruined, I'd be happy to buy you another."

"Neither will be necessary, but I do appreciate the offer. Why were you surprised I attended the gala?"

"I'm not sure, but somehow an art restoration expert and appraiser seemed an odd choice for a jewelry exhibit."

Think fast. He may not know anything, but he thinks there's something to know and that's just as bad.

"Mine is not the kind of business you advertise. I

often find new clients at events like the gala—museum directors, wealthy individuals, et cetera. You were providing security? I was surprised to see that the centerpiece for the exhibit is back."

"Our transport ran into trouble and had to return to London."

Transport? Interesting choice of words.

Claire said nothing but allowed him to lead her back into the gallery where the necklace was in its state-of-the-art protective case. As the jewelry exhibit was over, he led her to one of the paintings.

"What do you make of this?" he said, indicating a copy of the Mona Lisa. "Everyone knows the original hangs in the Louvre, so what's the point?"

"The point is that the Mona Lisa has been loaned out before for brief periods of time, but this is a digitized version. It is an attempt to show the difference in the colors we now see, versus those in the original. There are subtle differences, and the original has aged, but the result is remarkable."

"I would think an art restoration expert would find digitized reproductions especially distasteful."

"I do if they are being used to perpetrate a fraud, but if we could get this kind of technology into the hands of educators, imagine how it could positively impact younger children and their appreciation of the work of those who went before them."

He nodded. "What about 3D imaging, for say the necklace?"

"Again, depending on its purpose, I am not opposed to the idea. Transporting children to a museum has become more problematic, so I would think as a teaching tool those kind of advanced graphics capabilities would only increase their learning opportunities. How long will the necklace be staying in London?"

"I'm afraid I can't answer that because of security concerns. The owners agreed to let it be put on display here as frankly that case and the museum's added security make it probably the safest place in London. We believe someone might have been planning something during the gala, but nothing came of the rumors we've heard."

"There were rumors?"

Fletcher nodded. "Like those paintings, the necklace has a taint to its provenance. We heard that a notorious jewel thief might be making a second attempt."

"Second?" Shit, it sounded like Fletcher and his people might be on to something.

"Yes, we think there was an earlier attempt made. Combined with the rumors about last night, my concern is whoever it is may well try again. I want the thing back home with its owners in Paris."

She withdrew her hand. "It was nice talking with you, Mr. Fletcher…"

"Please call me, Fletch."

"I wasn't thinking of calling you anything at all."

"Get out of there," hissed Mia in her ear.

"And I was so hoping you might call me sweet-heart," he teased.

Claire tried to give him her best scowl, but when he waggled his eyebrows at her, all she could do was laugh.

"Do you ever just take no for an answer?"

"Rarely, and never if it's something I really want."

"Do I fall into the latter category?"

"Most assuredly. Take pity on the poor American in London. Let me take you to lunch at my hotel. Gordon Ramsay runs the Savoy Grill."

"No! No! No!" said Mia.

Thinking perhaps she could pump him for information, she smiled. "I suppose I could do that."

"Excellent. I'll have them send a car, and until then, why don't you take me to your favorite piece of art in the museum and educate me about all the things I don't know about."

"Abort! Abort! Abort," Mia practically screamed in her ear.

"Let me introduce you to eighteenth-century artist Henry Hogson. I think his landscapes are absolutely divine and so underrated. The museum has one of my personal favorites called The Parsonage."

With her hand now comfortably tucked into his arm, Claire led Fletch to one of the other galleries while Mia bemoaned and berated her in equal fashion. If she had been sure Fletch wouldn't see her,

Claire would have removed her earpiece. She adored Mia but Fletch might well be able to supply them with just what they needed in the way of information, and if she was lucky, might well scratch an itch that hadn't been scratched in a very long time.

CHAPTER 6

FLETCH

Fletch wasn't sure what it was, but he was damn sure there was something about Claire Mitchell that just didn't quite add up. She'd been here the other night. Surely, she would have seen the three paintings Pennington had wanted to show her. All of the paintings and other *objet d'art* that were currently on display at the museum had been listed on the program for the gala. He didn't quite buy her explanation that she had been mining the field for new business.

There was also the business about her face being obscured in the video footage. His tech said it might have been a fluke, might be a glitch in the camera footage or she could have been using some kind of a jamming device. The latter greatly amused him, as they had used a jamming frequency against whoever was after the necklace.

He wondered if the beautiful and alluring Claire Mitchell had lied to him. God, he hated liars. His ex-girlfriend had been a consummate liar and an actress, although not by trade. By trade she was an investment banker for one of the banks based here in London. Evangeline had all the right assets to be the perfect partner: she was beautiful, although a bit thin for his taste; she had a straight chic blonde bob, wore the most fashionable outfits, lived in killer stilettos, and had the perfect pedigree and connections. Unfortunately, once you moved past the surface, there was nothing of substance—only style and a façade.

He considered himself to be lucky to have escaped her clutches. She'd always wanted more from him than she, herself, was willing to give—financially and emotionally. She had also been incapable of fidelity. Getting back a day early from a business trip and wanting to surprise her had reaped rewards he had never imagined. On his way from Heathrow to her fabulous condo in Kensington, he had been imagining all the righteously nasty ways he wanted to fuck her.

Unfortunately, someone else had gotten there first —her assistant Gary. There had been no mistaking the sounds coming from Evangeline's bedroom. Skin slapping against skin, moaning, groaning, and Evangeline's breathy panting as she neared climax. He'd thought about confronting them, maybe punching Gary out, but realized her infidelity provided him with the perfect exit. He left the flowers he'd bought her on the foyer table with a note that read: 'I hope you and Gary will be happy together,' and then let himself out. What few things he had there, she was welcome to keep, toss, or destroy.

He'd been pretty much celibate for the past eighteen months. Well, celibate if you counted sex with a partner. If you counted your own hand, he'd had a rip-roaring sex life going on. In some ways, it was a lot easier; his hand didn't want a damn thing except to be washed in return.

Fletch had given Evangeline little thought after their breakup. After blocking her calls and texts, he'd had a single encounter with her as he'd left his farm. This had been no chance meeting, as his farm was far outside of London.

"Ry, you have to listen to me. Gary means nothing to me," she said as she chased after him.

Fletch didn't break stride, but also did not give her the satisfaction of speeding up. "I'm not sure how to tell you this, Evangeline, but that doesn't make it any better. In fact, I think I'd have more respect if you said you were madly in love with him…"

"In love with Gary? Don't be daft. He's just my assistant, and I was really jonesing for some dick."

He stopped, smiled and said, "And any dick would do. While I'm sure your father has always thought any cunt in the dark would do, I'm not sure he'd apply the same standard to you. What do you think?"

Fletch cocked his head and said nothing more. When Evan-

geline didn't either, he knew she understood that she'd put her foot in it and that he was done. The implied threat was silent and understood. When she said nothing and stepped back, he said, "Goodbye, Evangeline."

They'd never spoken again. He couldn't help but compare the cold and empty shell of Evangeline to the warm and vibrant woman who simmered next to him. In contrast, Claire was slightly messy, with dark curly hair, a skewed sense of fashion that seemed to suit her, and from what he had seen, the most gloriously curvy figure a man could ask for. She had breasts that were more than a handful, a cinched waist and generous hips a man could hold onto when he was taking her hard from behind.

Fletch knew she was talking; he was watching her luscious lips move. Instead of paying attention to what she was saying about some guy named Hogson, he was thinking of what they'd feel like against his own, or better yet, wrapped around his cock, which was signaling its approval of the lovely Claire Mitchell but wanting to straighten up and come to attention.

"Did you even hear a word I said?" she challenged him in an easy, bantering tone.

"Some guy named Hogson; English landscape artist; never recognized for his talent until after his death."

"Not one damn word."

"Is there more?"

"Quite a bit. What you just regurgitated to me is

what can be read about the artist in the little card by his painting. Care to tell me what you were thinking about?"

A man in a tailored suit tapped Fletch on the shoulder. How had that happened? It had been decades since anyone was able to sneak up on him, but then until this afternoon he hadn't had Dr. Claire Mitchell and her smokin' hot body to focus on.

"Mr. Fletcher, I'm from the Savoy. I have your car right outside when you're ready."

"Excuse me; I'm with Mr. Fletcher. Do you have to take us back to the Savoy?"

"No, ma'am. I've been assigned to him for the rest of the day. I'm happy to take you wherever you'd like."

"Is there somewhere you'd rather go than the Savoy?" asked Fletch, intrigued.

"Yes, there's a great little spot right on the Thames just outside the city. I swear it has the best food…"

"Haverty's?" said the driver.

Claire beamed at him. "That's the one."

The driver nodded. "The best fish and chips in London."

"I know, and their mushy peas are to die for," laughed Claire.

"What is it with you English and mushy peas? I've always had peas that had some bite to them," said Fletch.

"That's because you, sir, are an uncouth American with no taste in tuxedos."

Fletch laughed. "Okay, that's it. First, I take you to lunch; then you accompany me to get a proper tuxedo."

Before she could object, he swept her along toward the front door of the museum and into the waiting car.

Once the driver was inside, he caught Fletch's eye in the rearview mirror. "Haverty's, sir?"

"Whatever the lady wants."

"Careful, Fletcher, I might just hold you to that."

He pulled Claire a little closer to his body. "Sweetheart, you can hold anything of yours close to me anytime you want for as long as you want."

She extricated herself enough so that there was some distance between them, but there was no way to miss the uptick in her arousal—her pupils dilated, her skin took on a bit of a blush, and he was certain he could smell her scent. She was lucky they had a driver, and he had more control over his libido than either it or his dick liked. Were it not for those two conditions —the driver and his control, as opposed to his dick and his libido—he'd have had Claire on her back, that skirt rucked up past her hips and his face buried in her sex.

The drive to Haverty's was fairly quick and he could see people queued up to order. It was really nothing more than a glorified food truck with a lot of seating options. As they pulled up and the driver opened the door, the delicious aromas drifting toward them from the place were heavenly. There was nothing wrong with the Savoy Grill—the food and service were impeccable—but this was more the kind of place he'd pick for himself. He took people to the Savoy to impress them, but it pleased him more than it should have that Claire had picked this place instead.

After ordering fish and chips with mushy peas for her and fennel slaw for him, they scored a table for two right on the Thames that afforded them a little privacy. Fletch watched her tear apart the fish with her fingers, popping a bite-size piece into her mouth. When she'd grabbed a fork, he'd thought she would use it to eat her meal.

As she bit into a French fry or chip, as the Brits called it, she looked at him askance and said, "What?"

"I was afraid you were going to use a fork to eat your whole meal."

"You got a fork."

"Yes, but I knew it was only going to be for the fennel slaw."

He watched her as she watched him knock back a bottle of Otter Ale, another thing they had in common. Evangeline would never have taken a sip from a long-neck bottle with the kind of relish Claire did. There was the chief difference between them—

Evangeline experienced life; Claire *lived* it; in fact, she seemed to *revel* in it.

After taking a sip, he licked his lips and saw her eyes dilate. Maybe having lunch by the Thames instead of the Savoy had been a mistake.

"So, how did you come to found Silver Arrow Security, and what is it your firm does?"

"After three tours in the Middle East and realizing we were accomplishing nothing, I wanted out. I stopped in London on my way home and found myself in Devon. The country I had been in was stark and desolate, while Devon was lush and welcoming. I saw a 'for sale' sign on a farm that had gone fallow. Something about it called to me. So, I bought it and then began restoring it."

"So, you're a farmer in your spare time?" she asked with a laugh.

"Nothing wrong with being a farmer and working with your hands…"

Claire reached across and laid her hand on his arm. The connection between them sizzled. "You misunderstand. You're such a fascinating enigma— first that terrible tuxedo and then today you have on a pair of fine wool trousers paired with my guess is an Egyptian cotton shirt. You were in the military, prob- ably in special operations, and yet you seem more open than brooding."

She took his hand in both of hers and he stared as

she turned his over and rubbed her thumbs across the calluses. "You ride."

"Maybe I just work my fields."

"Nothing wrong with that, but those calluses come from riding a lot. I should know, I have a whole routine I go through to keep mine soft, including never riding without gloves. My granda raised me and he was the horse master and chauffeur for a wealthy peer. So never, ever apologize for those calluses."

Claire released his hand, leaned back in her chair, and took another bite of her fish.

He answered the unasked question. "I raise sport horses. It's slow going to get established as a breeder of horses that people really want to buy, but I'm working on doing just that. Security was a natural fit for me, so I founded Silver Arrow to pay the bills while I build a business and a reputation for breeding the best sport horses in the world."

"Not just Great Britain, but the world."

"Why settle for just an island when the whole world beckons?"

"Why indeed," she laughed. "How'd you get involved with the Grenadine Necklace?"

Had her mouth just tightened almost imperceptibly?

"Someone made an attempt to steal it while it was in the *Chateau des Templiers*. The owners had agreed to allow the museum to exhibit it over a year ago. They decided not to let the attempted theft deter them.

That's when the insurance company called in my firm to be on the premises and to transport it to and from the museum."

"Somehow I think you're more than a glorified courier."

"If I'm not, they are paying me way too much money."

Claire laughed—not just with her mouth, but with her eyes and her whole being.

"My firm is responsible for the safety of the necklace until it is returned back to the *Chateau des Templiers*."

She leaned in and looked around with a conspiratorial grin. "Do you really think someone would try again? I don't recall anything untoward happening at the gala. Did I miss something?"

Something about her casual questioning set off his alarm. He couldn't quite put his finger on it, but he chided himself to proceed with caution. "No. Nothing happened at the gala, but there had been word on the dark web that a notorious jewel thief had been behind the first attempt. There seemed to be signs that he would try again."

"Do you know who this thief is?"

He shook his head. "No. No one even knows enough to give him some catchy nickname."

"Does anyone know anything about him?"

"No, but as I was doing my research, I think I've spotted a pattern no one else has noticed."

"Oooh, like an MO—that's what they call it right?"

Her grin was infectious and he found himself reflecting it back to her. "MO stands for *modus operandi,* which means a particular way of doing something. He doesn't have that. He's come in through the ductwork, across an alley on a high wire, eluding laser traps, and a lot of other ways. He hits homes, banks, museums… wherever the jewels happen to be. Where I spotted the pattern is in what he steals."

"Well, if he's a jewel thief, wouldn't it stand to reason he steals jewels?"

"Yes, but only jewels with a sketchy provenance, and in particular pieces that were supposedly stolen by the Nazis.

"The Nazis?" she asked, shaking her head. "I think for some the Nazis are like bogeymen and people forget some of the horror they visited not just on the world, but on individuals who had lives and families. I don't know, sometimes I feel like I'm one of very few people who even cares anymore, and I ask myself why do I care. So many people seem to feel it was more than three-quarters of a century ago, so it doesn't matter."

There was something about the way she seemed to be trying to deflect it that didn't sit right. Deciding to see what kind of reaction he'd get, he continued, "I'm sure the people from whom they were stolen cared a great deal, as do their descendants. Most of them died in the concentration camps. He's bound to get caught at some point. I'd just like it to be me."

"Why?"

"Because there's a bounty on his head of ten million dollars."

Claire choked on something and had to take a gulp of ale to wash whatever it was down her throat. "Ten million?"

"Yeah, Lloyd's of London started the barrel rolling and then a bunch of the other insurance companies pitched in. They say that doesn't even touch what the standard finder's fee of ten percent would be if you added up everything he's stolen."

"More than one hundred million?"

He nodded. "And some of the pieces are truly priceless."

Her fingers wrapped around the bottle of Otter Ale as she brought it to her lips and took a long, slow swallow. He could almost see her throat relaxing under its cool effervescence and he wondered how it would react to a full load of his cum.

"I think I've seen a couple of news articles about some high-end master thief, but I never imagined he'd stolen so much, or that the insurance companies were so desperate to catch him. Do you think it ever bothers them that these people are recovering money on jewels that were never theirs in the first place?"

"No. They always have provenance that will cover them, but for the most part, they didn't steal the jewelry, they simply bought it from a broker who got it from those who got it from the victims."

"But how does once removed make it better?" She sat back again, clearly incensed.

"It doesn't. That's why they have the forged paperwork And some of these people acquire these tainted pieces of jewelry and art and never let it see the light of day."

"What does the thief do with it?"

"What do you mean?" he asked, snagging one of her chips.

"Well, by this time, doesn't he have enough money? And if so, then what truly motivates him? Maybe, just maybe, he's a kind of modern-day Robin Hood. Maybe whoever he is, he wants to see that those who lost so much have their property returned to them. Maybe he is making right those original sins by returning whatever he's stolen to those to whom it rightly belongs."

"Maybe, but that doesn't change the fact that he's stealing, himself. He too is robbing people of what legally—perhaps not rightfully or morally—belongs to them. The fact is, we live in a world where vigilante justice cannot be tolerated. I know it's a romantic way to look at life, but where do you draw the line? The whole slippery slope theory always wins out. If someone got away with a theft worth a thousand dollars, why not go to a hundred thousand, or a million?"

"But if he's not keeping the pieces for himself…"

"We don't know that he isn't, and even if we did, it wouldn't matter. It doesn't even matter if he believes himself to be right and just. It isn't his decision to make, regardless of how it makes people feel about it. If people feel that someone has something that was stolen from them, there are proper channels for them to go through to challenge someone's provenance and recover what they believe is rightfully theirs."

"Who? Who do they go to? There may be places to report it, but in the end the police are overworked, the insurance company doesn't want to lose out and the various commissions that were set up to deal with this have no teeth. They are powerless. I say let this thief, whoever he is, make right what was put so wrong by evil men."

God she was gorgeous when she was impassioned. He wondered what it would be like when her crystal blue eyes flashed and filled with passion and arousal for him?

She shook her head. "I don't know Fletch; I think you're gorgeous and there's a lot about you that appeals to me, but I think at the end of the day we're not all that suited to one another. Kind of like oil and water… or maybe even nitro and glycerin."

"I don't know how to tell you this, sweetheart, but nitro and glycerin get along just fine—it's the rest of the world that has to be careful about how they deal with them."

"Maybe, but you have a job to do, and I have a Hogson at home calling my name. The owners found it behind an old plow in the back of a barn. Thank you for lunch."

Claire stood and walked away from him and past their car and driver.

What went wrong? We were getting along so well. He looked up at her and could see her literally shut down. *What was she hiding?* The only thing he could think was that she knew more about the jewel heists than she let on. Could she be the thief's accomplice? She hadn't even been born when the first heists were pulled, but then again, whoever started had to be too old or dead to have been pulling off the heists over the past decade.

"Claire?"

She turned around. *Had she just tried to hide a look of sorrow?* "Yes?"

"You should know someone is going to catch the thief. And as there is a ten-million-dollar reward, I intend for that someone to be me."

CHAPTER 7

CLAIRE

"Shit! Shit! Shit," said Mia in her ear.

Apparently, Mia had heard everything. "I know," Claire said as soon as she could quietly talk into her hand and not attract attention. "We purposefully tried to change things up for each heist."

"Do you think he suspects you?"

"I think 'suspect' is too strong a word, and I don't think he has any idea I'm the actual thief. What I think is that he may believe I know more about it than I'm letting on. I should have kept my damn mouth shut about possible reasons why."

"You should have gotten the hell out of there and never gone to lunch. I'm on my way to your location. Are you walking east or west?"

"West. He has a driver from the Savoy so they should head east back into London proper. I don't

want him to see me get into a van with someone.
We'll need to make sure we're clear of him, and even
then, let's find an alley or secluded spot."

"Gotcha. What about that tunnel that runs under
the bridge? No one is ever around there; well, at least
not during the day."

"That should work. I should be there in about
half an hour. I'll keep looking for Fletch and the car
from the Savoy."

Claire picked up her pace, glad she'd worn her
riding boots. They were sturdy and comfortable and
made for rough terrain. She doubled back and crossed
the road several times to ensure she wasn't followed.
Fletch must have taken the hint—more's the shame.
He was all of the romantic dreams she'd ever had—
dominant, self-confident, authoritative, and a good
leader.

Very few people thought Claire capable of following, but the fact was, she craved it. The idea that she
could give up having to be in control all of the time
was like nirvana to her. No one believed because she
tended to challenge anyone who tried to control or
assert any kind of authority over her. It wasn't that she
wanted to be in control, she'd just never had much of
a choice. She longed for the day when there was a
man strong enough to draw a line in the sand. She'd
sensed that Fletch might just be that, but he would
never understand her need to steal. It was a promise
she'd made Poppi, and one she meant to keep.

And he was just her type physically—silky dark hair that had been deliberately and expertly cut for a slightly disheveled look or as though a lover had just run her hands through it. She realized now that his rumpled look from the night of the gala had most likely been a ruse. He had a gorgeous face—sexy, masculine with what seemed to be a permanent day's worth of scruff. He was tall and muscular, and he made her feel as though she was just the right size and feminine. She'd long ago realized that somewhere along the line she'd decided she was just 'too much' of a lot of things: height, boobs, hips, hair, all of it. But Fletch had made her feel sexy and vulnerable as though only he could keep her safe.

A small thrill had run through Claire's body when he'd tucked her hand into the crook of his arm—not once, but twice, and then had steered her into the car. It was all she could do, when he pulled her close, not to just snuggle in and inhale his scent. There had been a burgeoning intimacy between them—as if they understood each other on a whole other, visceral level that no one else could. It was intoxicating, thrilling, and dangerous.

Ten million dollars? Ten fucking million dollars? Maybe she should just offer to stop if they paid her—but then where would that leave all the countless victims who really had no other hope but her?

She picked up her pace and headed for the tunnel under the bridge. As Mia had predicted, there was no one there, but just to be safe, she took refuge in a small space behind one of the pillars—one where she couldn't be seen from the front or either side, with her back to a stone wall.

Hearing a vehicle approach she almost stepped out to flag Mia down, but as it slowed and rolled past her position, she realized it was the vintage town car from the Savoy. The windows were rolled down and she could see Fletch scanning what passed for a sidewalk on either side of the tunnel.

She heard another vehicle approaching and knowing how sound would carry, said very quietly, "That's Fletch. Don't even slow down, just keep going. Go back to your place and I'll meet you there."

"I can't just leave you here."

"You can and you will. They may have spotted the van the night of the gala. Park it at the warehouse and go home. I'll see you there."

"Claire…"

"Mia. Go. I'll be fine; there's an underground station not far from here."

"Okay. But keep your commlink open."

Claire smiled. She knew Mia worried, but only because she cared. She had adopted Claire's cause as her own and had been an invaluable partner. She often denigrated her contribution but Claire knew for a fact that without Mia, Claire would never have been able to pull off some of the heists they had.

After what seemed like an eternity, but was probably less than fifteen minutes, Claire could neither hear nor smell any vehicle in the tunnel. She cautiously stepped out of her hiding place. Seeing no one, she made her way quickly out of the tunnel, into town and down the steps to the underground. This was not normally a stop she gave any notice to, so she had to study the map to figure out which train to get on. Armed with that knowledge, she paid cash for a ticket and took the tube back into London, getting off two stops past the one closest to Mia's, buying a ticket for a train going back that way and then getting off one stop before. Sure that no one was following her, Claire trotted up the steps into the fading sun.

It was late afternoon, but she still had several hours before she needed to be home to feed the horses. She could always call a neighbor, but the less people knew about her comings and goings, the better. Finally, she knocked on Mia's front door. The great wooden door was flung open, and Mia hauled Claire in for a big hug while simultaneously closing it.

"Thank god, you're safe," she said breathlessly.

"It's not like he wants to kill me. He just wants to arrest me and collect the money. Promise if something goes wrong anywhere down the line and I'm not going to get away clean, you'll turn me in and collect the money."

"I will not."

Claire grinned. "I know, but I just thought I should put it out there. I had time to think on the way here. Come on, I want to look at the museum's blue-prints. Didn't you tell me you thought we'd overlooked something?"

"You had time to think? I was on the verge of throwing up, I was so worried."

Claire looked at Mia. "You don't have to do this. If this is too much for you, you should walk away."

"And you'll do what? Good god, there are times you can't get your computer to update properly. No, you're the one with the nerves of steel. I'm the one with the technological know-how. So, what did you think about other than the hunky Ryland Fletcher?"

"He is kind of dishy, isn't he? I almost forgot he was my adversary when we were having lunch like a couple of normal people. But normal isn't in the cards for me. Not for a long while to come."

"So, give. What are you thinking about doing that you know I'm going to hate?"

Claire grinned at her wickedly. "We're going to steal it tomorrow."

"We're going to steal what tomorrow? Because you can't mean the necklace. Fletcher and his team are in full force. The Yard has people undercover. They're expecting you—well, not you, but someone like you—to make another grab for it. And we don't have time to get in place tonight, and we…" Her voice trailed off as Claire nodded slowly. "You have lost your mind."

"Nope. You're right. No one is going to expect the thief to pull it off during the daylight. We know that they're trying your firewall—off the subject, but what are you going to do about that?"

"I'm going to lay a trap for them that'll burn down the wire and fry their system. Then we junk this computer and move to one of the backups."

"One of the backups? How many backups do you have?"

"More than enough to shut those bastards down, but let's go back to the part where we were talking about how batshit crazy you are."

"I am, but that's beside the point. I'm just going to walk in there and take it. You'll do something brilliant like set off the fire alarms—sprinklers and everything—that'll trigger them trying to get everybody out before the whole building shuts down. I can throw some smoke bombs if we need them to fuck up the cameras…"

"That's not going to work."

"Why not?"

"Because I can't get through the museum's firewall to get to the system."

"Not even to turn off the sound?"

"Nothing. I am completely shut out."

Claire started to laugh.

"What?" asked Mia.

"Oh my God," Claire laughed, trying hard to catch her breath.

"What?" asked Mia, the frustration beginning to come out in her voice.

Claire shook her head. "Sometimes I think we get so involved in how smart we are and how technologically advanced we are, that we forget it wasn't always that way. Can you remove that little jamming thingy from my headband and put it in something else?"

"Like what?"

"I dunno—a scarf, maybe a ball cap?"

"Sure. As long as it's not any thicker than the headband it should be fine. What are you thinking?"

"I'm thinking we go old-school. Fletch said no one's spotted the pattern because the MO isn't the same. This one should really throw him for a loop. Do you need to be through the firewall to hit them with an electronic pulse?"

"No," said Mia, shaking her head.

"Good. I'll go in to talk to Pennington and raise my concerns about the three paintings. It is perfectly characteristic of me to be a pain in the ass. Once I've done that, I'll go look at them again. They're in the gallery behind the necklace. You send an EMP…"

Mia nodded. "It'll disrupt the power to the whole building, including the alarms, the lights, the cameras, everything."

"I'll make sure I'm in place and when you say go, I'll cut a small hole in the case, reach in and snatch the necklace. I'll hide it somewhere on me—my bra, under a ball cap, we'll sew in a pocket, whatever…"

"The scarf; the vintage Hermes scarf I got you last year for your birthday. Didn't you buy something to wear with it?"

"I did. I can easily conceal the jammer in that. I'll grab the necklace and just walk out. It may not be fancy, but I'm pretty damn sure it'll work. Something that simplistic, when they know we were using advanced technology, will throw them off guard."

Mia grinned. "You may be certifiable, but I think this might work."

"I'll go in tomorrow to scope it out. We'll do it around lunchtime when lots of people are there. I'll make the call on the spot, and we'll get it done."

"I like it. Why don't we head out to your place so I can get the scarf fixed…"

"I can make dinner, have a lovely ride, and you can sleep over."

They packed up Mia's gear and bundled into her car. Mia made sure to drive in and around London before heading out to Claire's place. As they drove past the Savoy, Claire couldn't help but look at it longingly.

"You really like him, don't you?" asked Mia quietly.

"Yeah, but it could never work between us and my dropping my guard around him, even for a second, could spell disaster for us. No, I need to chalk up Ryland Fletcher to 'things that might have been.'"

"I'm sorry."

"So am I."

Mia was a good enough friend to know what giving Fletch up was going to cost her and so let her friend mourn her loss in her own way as they made their way out to Greenwich.

CHAPTER 8

CLAIRE

The next morning, Claire dressed casually, keeping in mind she was going to wear the scarf and secure it around her neck so that it would, if necessary, obscure her face. They drove into London and found a place for Mia to park where she would have a clear line of sight to the museum so that she could focus her EMP and disturb as few other buildings as possible.

Once she was in place and secure, Claire left the van and headed toward the museum, trotting up the steps and waving to the security guard as she headed for the reception desk.

"Dr. Mitchell, how nice to see you again."

"Thanks, I know I'm not on his schedule, but if I could have a few minutes of his time..."

"I know he has a lunch appointment, but I also know he'll make time for you."

Following behind the receptionist, Claire said, "This may be the last time he wants to make time for me."

The receptionist knocked on the door and stuck her head in saying, "Dr. Mitchell asked to speak with you."

"Show her in," he called, rising from his desk as Claire entered. "Always a pleasure, Dr. Mitchell.

"I hope you still think so after you hear what I have to say. I feel obligated to report those paintings to the authorities. I know that in the case of one of them, the descendants are actively seeking redress through the courts. They haven't known where the painting was, but now they will. I know you thought them to have legitimate provenance at first, but when you began to question it, you called me in."

Pennington nodded his head. Claire was fairly sure he understood she was giving him cover. She wanted him to be thinking kindly enough of her, that he wouldn't believe she could be a part of any theft.

"I just don't want you to get caught up in the middle of this thing. It has the potential to get very ugly, very quickly, and to become very public," she continued.

"Of course, I understand your position, as once you gave me your opinion, I knew what had to be done. Perhaps we could make a joint report to the Commission."

"What an excellent idea, Edgar. You don't mind if

I call you Edgar, do you? And you must call me Claire."

"I would be delighted."

"What if I draft it, you review it, and if it represents what we both want, we'll sign it and have it delivered?"

"That is an excellent idea. I want to thank you for allowing me to go on record as opposing this sort of thing. There's far too much of it going on in the art world."

"I agree. Those of us with our ethics intact need to stand together." Claire reached out and shook his hand. "Thank you again, Edgar."

"It is my pleasure, Claire."

She turned away and left his office and headed back to where the paintings were hanging. Edgar Pennington would be the first person to defend her, saying it was only natural for her to want to see them again before drafting such an important report.

See? All you have to do is give people the opportunity to do the right thing, and most of them will.

She wandered through the museum, taking her time, but ensuring she knew the position of all the security personnel and cameras. She went into the gallery where the questionable paintings were hanging and made a quiet show of looking at all of them more closely. She'd searched high and low for Fletch and not seen him. *Now or never.*

Moving into position she muttered under her

breath. "Getting into position. On my mark. Shit, Mia, this is going to work."

"Shut up, and let's get this over with before I have a heart attack."

"In position. In three-two-one-now."

Mia did her thing, sending an EMP and disrupting the power—turning off the lights and cutting the energy supply to the alarms. Claire breached the secure area around the necklace's case and when nothing happened, cut a small hole in the rear glass and lifted the necklace, putting it beneath the scarf around her own neck. She replaced it with a cheap replica of colored glass that Mia had purchased at the beginning of the exhibit. Moving away from the case, she stepped beyond the cordoned-off area, hooking the velvet rope back into place. In and out in under sixty seconds.

Just as the lights came up, Claire joined a small group of people heading towards the exit at the front of the building. She strolled out slowly with the group, nonchalantly nodding to the security guard who moved in and stared suspiciously around the room. No one would notice the hole in the back of the case for a while, she hoped.

It had been laughably old-school and incredibly risky, but it had worked. She had the Grenadine Necklace and vowed to herself that she would see it back in the hands of the rightful owners before the end of the week.

"Heads up. The dreamboat is entering the building and there are cops headed to the museum."

Claire offered her arm to an older woman as they approached the stairs. "Lean on me and we'll get you out of here. No use you taking any risk."

She may have been talking to the elderly lady, but the message was meant for Mia.

"You need to get out of there. If you get caught up in that group still inside, they'll detain you."

Claire heard him before she spotted him. "An EMP? How the fuck did that happen?" snarled Fletch.

She couldn't hear the response but focused her attention on the woman whose group seemed to have deserted her. "Who are you with?"

"My family. See?" she said pointing to where they were standing, scanning the steps looking for her. "Bless you for your kindness in helping me negotiate those steps."

"It was my pleasure," Claire assured her.

"Claire?" called Fletch.

She turned around giving him her most dazzling smile. "Fletch, I was hoping I might see you and apologize for the way I took off."

He took her arm, giving her cheek a kiss that sizzled along her skin. "I can't really talk, but I want to. Did you come to see me?" he asked, his voice taking on an edge of anxiety she hadn't expected.

She laughed. "No, you arrogant bastard, I came

to see Pennington and told him I felt it was imperative that we inform the Commission. He agreed with me and I'm going to draft a joint memorandum to them, but I was hoping at least to give you my apology."

"I was hoping for more than that," he teased.

When she said nothing, he pressed her. "Agree to have dinner with me," he said impulsively.

"I don't know, Fletch."

"I do. I'll be sure enough for both of us. I've got to get inside…"

The alarm from within the museum rang out, momentarily startling her. Instinctively she raised her hand to touch the scarf that concealed the stolen necklace.

"Please, sweetheart, say yes," cajoled Fletch.

She hesitated, but then relented. "But preliminarily only to dinner."

"Preliminarily," he said with a smile.

"What time?" she asked.

"Can we play it a little loose? I have a feeling I may be a while."

"Why?"

"The alarm bell?" he said, giving a nod to the museum. "I have a sneaky suspicion the bell tolls for me."

"Fletch! Fletch!" said the man she'd spotted as part of the security detail early on. "Thank God you're here. It's gone."

"Fuck."

Claire grabbed a pen out of her purse, turned Fletch's hand palm up and wrote her cell number on it. "I'll stay in the city. I can find a place to work and start drafting the memo. You go do whatever it is you need to do. If it's going to be too late, just let me know."

He nodded. "First chance I get, I'll text you so you have my number as well. Will Pennington vouch for you?"

She nodded as she considered the use of the word 'will' versus the use of the word 'can,' where an alibi was concerned. She was fairly sure she had covered her tracks and might only have been exposed for a fraction of a second.

"Good." He kissed her cheek again. "We'll get his statement and if we need more, I'll call you."

"If you're sure," she said, gazing into his eyes.

"I've never been more sure about anything in my entire life."

He kissed her again, this time on the lips. The first kiss was just a quick taste, before he hauled her in his arms and kissed her properly, holding her by her upper arms as he fused his lips to hers and she was able to feel the hard length that throbbed between them.

This put a bit of a wrinkle into her plans, but she thought in the end the whole thing had gone rather well. She watched him run up the stairs before pausing at the top. Claire raised her hand in a little wave and then blew him a kiss, which he caught and pressed to his lips with a smile. She watched him run into the museum before turning away and heading into the city. As she walked, the sirens of several police cars and mobile units split the afternoon sky as they raced towards the place of the jewel thief's latest heist.

CHAPTER 9

FLETCH

*W*as that really her? It was. But who had been the woman with her last night? After she'd left him at Haverty's, he'd gone looking for her, directing the driver to start driving a search pattern.

"I doubt she's going to walk all the way back into London, but there's an underground station that takes you right back into the city."

"Where?" Fletch asked.

"Back that way," the driver said, pointing.

They headed into the village. It never ceased to amaze Fletch how close small, quaint villages were to London itself. Sure, there were plenty of highways, but just off them, down a country road, quintessential cozy hamlets could be found. A check with the underground station attendant revealed no one had purchased a ticket, nor had a woman matching Claire's description used a pass or even entered the station.

"You've got it bad, son," said the older man who sold tickets and kept his eye on things to ensure no one rode for free.

"What do you mean?"

The man looked at him and grinned. *"No man describes a woman in that kind of detail or in those kinds of glowing terms unless he's gone off the deep end for her. Don't get me wrong; if you feel that way, go after her. Don't let her get away. My Emily did that. She was convinced she was going to be a big movie star, but I didn't give up. I chased after her with all my friends saying I was pussy-whipped. Maybe I was. I just knew I wasn't going to give her up. When I finally found her, some 'casting director' was trying to have his way with her. I put an end to that, gathered her up, and brought her home."*

Fletch smiled. *"I hope you punched the guy."*

"I beat the little shit to within an inch of his life. Emily and I have been happily married for close to fifty years. We have three children and seven grandchildren. It hasn't always been easy. We've had our share of fights, but it's been worth it. So, like I said, go find your girl."

"Thanks, I'll do that."

He'd gone back out to the driver. *"Not there; hasn't been there. Any thoughts?"*

"Not really, but we can do one of those grid searches."

Fletch grinned and leaned back in his seat. Where the hell had she gotten herself off to?

"What's that?" Fletch asked, pointing towards a little piece of what passed for the main road that seemed to dip down over the small overpass they were on.

The driver followed the road as it curled down and went

back under the road they'd been on. His driver slowed and Fletch rolled down the two back windows so he could see without the obscurity of the heavily tinted glass. He searched the area and could find no sign of her.

Sitting back, he sighed. "She's not here. I'm not sure where she is or how she got there, but she's gone. Let's head back to the Savoy."

Once back at the venerable hotel, he'd gone up to his room, changed into jeans, a sweater, and a pair of cowboy boots and taken the underground back out to Greenwich. She had to come home sometime.

He located her house with the use of his cell phone, several articles he had showing pictures of her house, and her home address that he'd obtained through one of his Scotland Yard contacts. He was there when a car not belonging to Claire had turned up and she and her friend had exited the car and gone inside.

He watched for the better part of the evening before deciding they were in for the night and heading back into London. He managed to snap a picture of her friend and had given it to his tech guy, Carter Hall, to put it through facial recognition. This morning, the identification of the woman had come back— Mia Kelly. She had no record, not so much as a speeding ticket. Fletch had set his guy to find what he could.

There wasn't much there. The only interesting tidbit had been that Mia and Claire had been roommates at a Swiss boarding school. Nothing to raise an eyebrow there. Mia Kelly was old money from Irish nobility. Mia's job, as far as anyone could tell was, as a freelance software tech.

Fletch was headed into the museum as numerous people seemed to be exiting. He caught sight of Claire as she helped an elderly lady down the stairs. With the throng of people, it would have been hard for the woman Claire was assisting to reach one of the handrails, so instead, she allowed Claire to assist her.

He made his way toward Claire, finally catching hold of her arm as she reunited her charge with the woman's family. He was able to grasp her arm before she could get away. Leaning down he bussed her cheek with his lips, inhaling her intoxicating scent. The old man at the station had been right; he had developed a real thing for Claire. He needed to get inside, yet he had been drawn to her like steel to a magnet; or was it more like a moth to a flame?

"I can't really talk, but I want to. Did you come to see me?" he said, hoping he didn't sound quite as desperate and hopeful to her as he did to himself.

She laughed. "No, you arrogant bastard, I came to see Pennington and told him I felt it was imperative that we inform the Commission about the paintings. He agreed with me and I'm going to draft a joint memorandum to them, but I was hoping at least to give you my apology."

"I was hoping for more than that," he said,

thinking *so much more than that*. "Agree to have dinner with me."

He'd been hoping to engage her interest for the afternoon, take her to dinner at the Savoy and then get her upstairs to his room, get her naked, and fuck her so hard she wouldn't be able to walk tomorrow morning. He'd had a miserable night, tossing, turning, and missing her, which was stupid. How could he miss having her in bed to make love to all night when he had yet to have her? That was going to change today if he had anything to say about it.

"I don't know, Fletch."

She seemed unsure, when she'd seemed so sure before. Why was that? What had caused this reversal in his fortune.

"I do. I'll be sure enough for both of us. I've got to get inside…"

The alarm started to sound, blaring its clarion call for all to hear. Now what? *This cursed necklace was going to be the end of me*, he thought as his dick throbbed. Being around Claire seemed to have that effect on him.

Claire seemed unsure of herself or how to respond in a way that she hadn't before. What had her on the edge and how could he use that to his advantage?

"Please, sweetheart, say yes," cajoled Fletch. Had she caught his use of the endearment?

"But preliminarily only to dinner."

"Preliminarily," he said with a smile, thinking once he had her at the Savoy, he'd be able to persuade her to come upstairs with him.

"What time?" he asked, not wanting to lose his momentum, but being reminded by the shrieking alarm that he needed to focus on the job and not on the woman he recognized was quickly becoming his obsession.

"Can we play it a little loose? I have a feeling I may be a while."

"Why?" she asked, seeming to be more interested in him than the alarm that was sounding.

"That alarm bell?" he said, giving a nod to the museum. "I have a sneaking suspicion the bell tolls for me."

He could feel her teetering on the edge of whether to agree or not, when one of his men came running down the stairs. "Fletch! Fletch! Thank God, you're here. It's gone."

"Fuck." His dick's reaction to this possible end to his plans was even less polite.

Before he could think how to respond, Claire grabbed a pen out of her purse, turned his hand palm up and wrote her cell number on it. "I'll stay in the city. I can find a place to work and start drafting the memo. You go do whatever it is you need to do. If it's going to be too late, just let me know."

She was coming! She was coming! Not yet his dick reminded him, but she will once I'm through with her.

If possible, his dick was even more excited and happy than the rest of him.

He nodded. "First chance I get, I'll text you, so you have my number as well. Will Pennington vouch for you?"

Fletch prayed she'd say yes. The pieces of the puzzle of the mysterious jewel thief were falling into place, and he didn't like the picture they seemed to be forming. He hadn't been able to stop himself from hinting that she might need an alibi, depending on what the video footage showed and what his people had seen.

Claire nodded.

"Good." He kissed her cheek again. "We'll get his statement and if we need more, I'll call you."

"If you're sure," she said, gazing into his eyes.

"I've never been more sure about anything in my entire life."

He kissed her again, this time on the lips. He'd meant to only press his lips to hers for the merest fraction of a second, but her mouth was far too tempting. He hauled her into his arms, his mouth descending on hers in a fierce, fiery, and all too fleeting kiss. Holding her close enough so that she could feel his erection throbbing between them, he kissed her properly—his lips demanding hers submit to him so that he could taste and explore.

Fletch forced himself to release her before following his man up the stairs to deal with whatever bullshit was cock blocking him. He paused at the top of the stairs to turn and look at her. Claire raised her hand in a little wave and then blew him a kiss. He pretended to catch the kiss and press it to his lips like some romantic idiot.

He turned to head into the building as the distinctive sound of police sirens began to fill the air. It was going to be a long afternoon. Claire's being here when whatever had happened had happened didn't bode well and only locked in another piece of the puzzle.

His team was waiting just inside the door. "What do we have?" he asked.

"The necklace is gone. We had some kind of disturbance in the power flow," answered one of his men.

"The EMP?" Fletch asked of no one in particular.

"Yes," answered Carter as he ran up to join them. "We were hit with an EMP. So simple; so easy. They didn't have to get past any of our security measures, just aim the pulse at our building and everything went down."

"For how long?"

"Couldn't have been more than ninety seconds."

"They had to have planned this," said the first man. "Whoever it was just walked up to the case, cut a hole in the back and swapped out the necklace for a cheap imitation. We've shut down the building and are starting to question people. The Yard's been called, and as you can hear, are joining us now."

"Did you have time to review the camera footage?" he asked.

Carter nodded. "Yep, that's why I was late. There's nothing. I spotted some movement, but that weird glitch we saw the night of the gala is back. I'm convinced someone is using a device that obscures their face and other details of the person wearing it. But I can see enough in the halo effect to believe it's a woman."

Fletch felt as though he'd been punched in the gut as all the pieces of the puzzle came together.

"Let's start questioning people. I'll coordinate working with the Yard." As his people went to do their business, he grabbed Carter's arm. "Run a deep background and detailed timeline for Claire Mitchell…"

"That cute little art restoration expert you've had your eye on?" Fletch nodded. "Anything in particular?"

"Check to see who the guy that raised her was. She indicated he was her grandfather and worked as a horse master. I need to know if either of them had any past criminal associations and/or a connection to looted Nazi treasure."

"On it," Carter said, turning to rejoin his computer.

"And send me the security feed from around the time of the heist."

She'd done it. There was no doubt in his mind about it. Claire had stolen the fucking necklace and probably every other piece of jewelry. She wasn't old enough to have performed the first heists, and yet, it had to be her. She was the only one emerging from all the data that he'd gathered that made all the pieces of the puzzle fit.

His cell buzzed and Fletch looked down to watch the camera footage. Everything looked fine. He watched as Claire walked past the diamond without so much as a glance. She was headed for the gallery where the three paintings were hung. A blip and everything in the footage went dark as the camera cut off. Less than ninety seconds later, the camera came back online just in time for him to see Claire walking unhurriedly from the room that housed the necklace.

Fletch could feel the muscle tick in his jaw. What the hell was she thinking? How the hell were they supposed to have a life together if she was in prison? Role-playing conjugal visits might be fun, but in reality, it would suck. He realized he wanted more than just sex with Claire; he wanted a life. Resolving to do whatever it took to make his fantasies become reality —regardless of whatever 'it' was and however 'it' had to play out, he vowed to himself to take care of it.

CHAPTER 10

FLETCH

letch leaned back against one of the
pillars close to the case which had once
contained the Grenadine Necklace. Fuck! She'd done
it. He was sure of it. Whatever the gizmo was that
had obscured the thief and made a halo around most
of her body might have disguised her enough to fool
everyone else, but he knew it was her. He knew it.
That little criminal had played him—or had she?
Whether she was the thief, or at least very involved,
was not in question, but why she'd done it, whether
she was acting alone, and whether she had used him
were yet to be resolved.

It had been a long, long afternoon. He'd met with
Scotland Yard and had negotiated a way to work with
them, allowing his team to take the lead. He was now
juggling how to maintain his working relationship
with the Yard, keep his team doing what he needed

them to do without getting them focused on Claire, and figure out how to keep Claire out of prison for a good portion of the rest of her life.

He didn't even think the United Kingdom allowed conjugal visits and he was damn sure not going to do without her while she served a prison term. Claire might not know it but Fletch was about to rock her world—in more ways than one. He would put an end to her thievery; she would walk the straight and narrow from now on, even if that meant handcuffing her to the headboard when he couldn't actively have eyes on her.

Come to think of it, that might be kind of fun.

Focus!

He looked at the palm of his hand. Surely, she wouldn't have given him her phone number if she didn't want him to help. She must have known he would figure it out. He texted her.

> Meet you for dinner at seven at the Savoy Grill

Claire's reply was a thumbs up emoji. So far, so good. That would give her time to go out to her place and feed her horses. He called the restaurant and made a dinner reservation—corner table at the back by the window. He was going to need a little privacy to get her set up, not only for a night of scintillating sex, but to let her know he expected her to return the Grenadine Necklace. Or maybe he should wait until she was asleep, search for it, find it, and return it to its owners, taking her to task privately. There were a lot of ways she could make it up to him—most of them involving his dick and some part of her sexy body.

At the end of a long day, Fletch made his way back to the Savoy and up into his room. He wanted to grab a quick shower while he figured out what to wear. Part of him wanted to look suave and dapper for her, but if he planned to search her house, the best way to get her to take him home was to be in jeans and boots.

As he stripped out of his clothes, his painfully hard dick reminded him that it had plans for their evening, as well, and they didn't necessarily include romancing their target or searching her home. No, what his dick wanted was to be shoved deep inside her and remain there until it fell off. His dick tended to be overly dramatic about these things, but never more so than when contemplating having Claire.

As he stood under the rainfall showerhead with the body sprays pulsing away, all he wanted to do was pound his head against the tile. How the hell had he let himself get caught up in all of her? He had never felt this way about a woman, never. He turned the water from hot to cold—as cold as he could stand it. Goosebumps started to cover his body, but did that affect the stiffness of his dick? Not even a little bit. It gleefully pulsed in anticipation of getting inside Claire. It had never been this unruly. Even as a teenage boy, Fletch had been able to control the damn thing. But not now. No, his cock was firmly in control, to the point a drop of pre-cum dripped onto the shower floor.

Regardless of how cold the water was, his dick knew Claire and her pussy would be hot—so very hot. It wasn't that Fletch disagreed with his dick, he just needed the thing to behave if he was going to be able to think through everything that needed to happen for them to have their own happily ever after.

'Happily ever after?' When did I start thinking in romantic terms?

Did he want to save Claire from herself? Yes. Did he want to fuck her so hard she never thought to step out of line again? Most definitely yes.

There were a lot of things to consider. Things like how to return the Grenadine Necklace and anything else she had in her possession without implicating her. Things like how he ensured she never stole again— although the idea of handcuffing her to their bed did have some merit. Things like making sure he could broker a deal that would keep her and her friend Mia safe and out of prison. Things like figuring out why the hell she'd done it, and who had done it before her?

Eighteen months of nothing but celibacy or his hand was about to come to a screeching halt. He'd figure out all he needed to do, and he would keep her safe. If the Yard, the insurance companies, bounty hunters, or anyone else got too close, he would take Claire and run. They'd disappear. Maybe buy a large sailboat and cruise the waters of the world until he could figure something out. But one way or another, her thieving was going to end, and they would be together.

'Now!' throbbed his cock. 'Now!'

He shook his head. There was no help for it. He needed to get his dick to settle down until they got through dinner, and he could get her alone. Then he would take the leash off his dick and the damn thing could go to town. He soaped up his hand, wrapped it around his cock, and began to stroke. His hand, no matter how slick and slippery, was no replacement for Claire's soaking pussy, but it would have to do. He had to stay in control of the situation if he was going to save her. And he had to save her.

Applying a bit more pressure, he leaned his head back and began to stroke faster, acknowledging his dick's whining about Claire's pussy feeling so much better. He had to agree. He closed his eyes and imagined what it would be like to have Claire in the shower with him, impaled on his cock as he thrust in and out of her, her pussy spasming all up and down his length. He'd use the wall of the shower for leverage and fuck her until she was either screaming his name or biting down on his shoulder to keep from doing so. He would fuck into her until she came at least twice, and he could drive deep, grinding himself against her as he filled her completely.

His entire body clenched in orgasmic bliss as his warm seed spilled onto the floor of the shower. He continued to stroke himself until he didn't have anything left. The climactic storm over for a moment, he leaned forward, resting his forehead against the cold tile. His body relaxed and his breathing became more regular. He increased the temperature of the water and let it beat against his muscles as he retook control of his unruly cock.

Stepping from the shower, he toweled off and chose to go with jeans, boots, and a sweater Evangeline had given him. She might have been an unfaithful bitch, but she did have great taste in clothing. He thought about shaving his five o'clock shadow but decided he wouldn't mind seeing a bit of beard burn along the inside of Claire's thighs. The face looking back from the mirror had a decidedly wicked grin. She might be a thief, but from now on she would be his thief, and the only thing she would be stealing was his heart.

As Fletch headed down to the lobby to wait for Claire, his cell phone buzzed. He glanced down. It was Carter.

"Fletcher," he chuckled, "but since you're calling me, you probably knew that."

"I did, indeed. I'm working on that deep background you had me do on Claire Mitchell…"

"Anything interesting?"

"The fact that there isn't nearly as much there as I would have thought and I'm having trouble finding content that isn't readily available to anyone is interesting in and of itself. It's as if someone has pulled a shroud over different parts of her life, but two things came to mind. I want you to know I would never share anything I tell you with anyone else."

"I know that."

"No, I mean, normally we share stuff with the team, and I may be out of line, but I got the distinct impression there was something going on between you and Dr. Mitchell. Something that has nothing to do with business. You can tell me I'm out of line…"

"You're not. In fact, I'm glad my tech guy actually has people skills and good instincts. So, what is it you think I need to know that you don't want to tell me."

"Her grandfather was Seamus O'Donnell."

"Why is that name familiar to me?"

"Famous master thief. Did a stretch in a prison outside of Belfast."

"I remember. He served his whole sentence because he wouldn't disclose where any of the stolen property went or who else might be involved."

"There were some that think his son-in-law might have been his accomplice. Seamus became Claire's guardian when someone forced the car that she and her parents were in off the road. She was thrown clear while buckled into her baby seat. Her parents perished, and Seamus went on the straight and narrow. Got a job with Sir Godfrey Robbins." Carter let the name hang in the air.

"Evangeline's father?"

How the hell had he missed that connection? Evangeline had spoken about Claire, although only in derisive terms, but the Claire that Evangeline had described bore little resemblance to the beautiful, sexy Dr. Mitchell.

"I'm afraid so. The girls weren't close…"

"I am aware." He recalled with startling clarity Evangeline's comments about the horse master's daughter. "The kindest thing Evangeline ever said about her was that she was an excellent rider, but a chubby ragamuffin."

"Claire Mitchell is a lot of things, but I wouldn't call her a chubby ragamuffin."

"Nor would I."

"But how the hell does someone like Seamus O'Donnell end up working for Robbins? And how did he afford that fancy Swiss boarding school? And the horses?"

"Claire mentioned her grandfather was a horse master for a peer, but not which one."

"You don't suppose she knew about you and Evangeline, do you?"

"I doubt it. I wasn't high enough profile for her. We didn't get the press coverage she wanted."

"Didn't she know that the paparazzi knows to keep their distance from you?"

"I might not have mentioned that. But what the hell would Sir Godfrey want with an ex-con Irishman? That is completely out of character for him. Keep digging and see what you can find."

"Will do. Do you think Dr. Mitchell might be involved?"

"If she is, she won't be for long."

"Got it. Let me know if I need to get rid of anything electronically."

"Thanks, Carter. I appreciate that."

Fletch ended the call and took the elevator down to the lobby. So, Claire was Seamus O'Donnell's granddaughter. That could go a long way toward explaining how she had become a master thief, herself.

As he entered the lobby of the Savoy, he saw her waiting demurely close to the front door, as if she could make a hasty retreat or escape if needed. She looked stunning. Someday he would have to tell her that he much preferred her in her bohemian outfits to her high society cocktail dress. But he rather imagined he'd prefer her in no clothes at all.

The dress was a combination of saturated colors in barn red and olive green, which contrasted beautifully with her long, dark, curly hair. His cock tightened at the thought of sinking his fingers into her silky mane and feeling some of it tickle his thighs while he guided her mouth to his staff. The maxi dress had an open front design from the knees, which allowed the shimmering, gossamer-like fabric to trail behind her like a billowing cloud. The bodice was fitted, with tiny buttons all up the front to the deep V neckline, and the beautiful three-quarter sleeves had no lining. The dress was subtle in its impact. It wasn't tight or cut too low or too high, but it made the most of everything Claire's figure had to offer.

He smiled broadly as he crossed to her. He wondered if she had any idea how truly beautiful she was. How she had remained single and unattached was beyond him. He meant to change both of those statuses as soon as possible.

He shook his head a little. When had marriage and forever become a part of his crystalized dream of Claire? Sure, he wanted to get her into bed, and he thought there was a very real possibility that they could make a life together, but suddenly Fletch wanted it all—the ring, the wedding, maybe even some kids if she wanted. He could even see himself breeding great horses for her to compete on internationally.

Fletch took her hand in his, bringing it up to his lips to kiss. "You look gorgeous. I'm surprised I didn't have to fight my way through throngs of men throwing themselves at you and professing their undying love."

The smile that lifted her lips wasn't demure or shy.

It lit up her entire face and was most easily seen in her twinkling blue eyes. "Hardly. Around here, I'm pretty much second shelf if not chopped liver."

He linked his arm with hers as he started toward the restaurant. "I hope you don't mind the Savoy. The food is excellent, and it's a great place to sit and talk."

"I've always wanted to come here, but it felt out of my league. I'm not, as you might have guessed, much of a fashionista."

"I think you are so far above all these mere mortals that they should bow down as you walk past."

Claire laughed. "You remind me of Poppi, my granda. He used to always say stuff like that, especially when some of the other girls teased me and hurt my feelings."

"Where are these girls? Let's have them hauled off to the Tower."

"You're kind of sweet when you're off duty. I'd tell you that you're gorgeous, but I don't want you to get a swollen head."

She had no way of knowing it, but the only swollen head he had was at the end of his engorged cock.

Fletch said nothing as they entered the restaurant and were shown to their table.

"As you've never been here, let me order for you. Anything you don't like?"

"Mushrooms, broccoli, cauliflower, and olives."

"Got it. What would you like to drink?"

"Water with ice would be great."

"No wine?"

"I'm afraid not. I'm pretty much a water, beer, and Diet Coke girl with the occasional shot of tequila."

He turned to the waitress. "We'll have the Beef Wellington with pomme puree and glazed carrots. We'll each have a house salad and start with splitting the Arnold Bennett soufflé. We'll both have ice water and the Meantime Anytime Ale with our main course."

"I think I like having someone order for me," she said, relaxing back into the chair.

"I think you'd find you like having someone do things for you, or at least share them if you tried."

"Maybe," she said, nodding slowly.

The soufflé was out quickly, and the waitress cut it in half and served it on individual plates.

When she walked away, Claire grinned. "I don't think she would have approved if we'd just dug into this thing with both our forks."

"Probably not, but what do we care what she thinks."

"True enough."

They talked and asked each other about their pasts, their current lives, and even touched on their future plans. He noted Claire tried to steer the conversation back to him while answering very carefully about her own.

After the beef Wellington had been served, he leaned forward, "Aren't you going to ask me about what happened at the museum?"

"I suppose I thought if it was interesting, and you could talk about it, you would tell me," she answered noncommittally.

"It seems that while you were in the museum, and both Pennington and the receptionist thought you were in Pennington's office, the Grenadine Necklace was stolen just moments before we ran into each other."

"You don't say," she said, taking a bite of the beef Wellington. "This is delicious. So, somebody nabbed it in broad daylight?"

He nodded. He had to give it to her, she was a cool customer. "There was a power fluctuation that left the museum without any kind of electricity for about ninety seconds. We think that disruption was caused by an EMP…"

"EMP?" she asked.

"Yes, an electromagnetic pulse. Doesn't really hurt anything, just overwhelms systems, causing them to reset and then come back online. By the time my people got to the case with the necklace, someone had cut a hole in the back and swapped out a cheap imitation for the real thing, and then presumably just walked out."

"That was pretty brazen. I thought jewel thieves only worked at night."

"Most do, but brazen is the right word. I suspect whoever it was knew a lot about the security system. I think I might have mentioned, we've been detecting cyber encroachments on the system for weeks, and we thought we had them shut out. I think when they figured out they couldn't come at us with some high-end hack, they decided to go old school. It was brazen and brilliant."

"You almost sound like you admire him."

"Not what he does, but I think there's a greater goal than money behind it. Like we talked about at lunch, I don't like vigilante kinds of justice, but it doesn't mean I don't respect the reason they're doing it."

"So, in your mind, the ends don't justify the means."

"Rarely, if ever."

"What if someone has no recourse?"

"There's always another recourse—a legal one. It might be expensive and time consuming, but what makes it right for one person to steal and not another?"

"I guess that's just something we will never agree about. I think certain wrongs need to be righted, and sometimes the only way, and I do mean the *only* way for a person to get justice, is if either they or someone else seizes it from those in power. I probably should get back to my place. Will you be staying in London?"

"Would you like it if I stayed in London?"

"And back to being an arrogant prick." She shook her head. "Just because I asked you a friendly question doesn't mean I'm dying to go to bed with you."

"God, I hope not. Necrophilia has never been an interest of mine. But I would very much like to take you to bed."

She stood up, laying her napkin on her plate. "And if wishes were horses, then beggars would ride."

"Is that how your granda afforded your riding career? By wishing it so?"

She extended her hand. "Thank you for dinner, Fletch. I hope you find what it is you want."

Before he could even get up, she'd spun on her heel and headed out the door. He hurried after her, leaving a cash gratuity on the table and stopping long enough to have the dinner charged to his room.

"Claire, wait up," he called after her as she pushed through the door. He wasn't long after her and was able to hail a cab. "I don't know about your grandfather, but mine taught me how to treat a lady when you take her to dinner."

"Really? Your grandfather thought you should invite her to the hotel's fancy restaurant and then take her to your room?"

He chuckled. "Point taken. My apologies if I offended your sensibilities."

As the cab pulled in to take her home, Fletch pulled her close but gave her a gentlemanly kiss on the lips. When he pulled back, he saw the look of disappointment and irritation flash through her eyes. He helped her into the cab and then on impulse, followed her in.

"Excuse me?" she asked, feigning indignation, but not very well.

"Sweetheart, I would make every excuse for you."

"Not what I meant, and you know it. Why did you get in the cab with me?"

"Because if you're not coming upstairs with me, I'm going to your place. The question has never been if we were going to fuck, but rather where we would fuck. So, as you weren't inclined to have it be the Savoy, and my place is all the way out in Devon, I suppose that means it'll be your place in Greenwich."

"And what if I want to go to Devon?" she asked with a bemused expression.

"That's fine with me, as long as our cab driver doesn't mind if we fuck in his back seat because there's no way I'm waiting more than three hours to get inside you."

Taking his face in her hands, she gave the cab driver her address and swung her leg over Fletch to straddle his lap. With an earthy chuckle, the cab driver pulled away from the Savoy and into traffic, en route to Greenwich.

CHAPTER 11

CLAIRE

*C*laire wasn't sure what made her climb into his lap but taking his face in her hands and fusing her lips to his in a fiery kiss, for all its newness felt so right and like they'd been kissing for years. She rubbed herself against him, loving how his hard cock pulsed between them.

"I'm clean and protected," she whispered as her mouth hovered over his.

"Same."

His hand ran up the front of her dress and unbuttoned the tiny buttons holding it together. His hand brushed against her lace-covered breast before unfastening the front closure and exposing it. Her nipple was pebbled, and she pressed her flesh into his hand as his mouth closed over hers. She had thought sitting in his lap would put her in control—she couldn't have been more wrong.

Heat and arousal surged through her system, empowering her and yet making her feel vulnerable at the same time. At first his mouth was sweet, gentle, coaxing, but as she moaned and sagged into his strength, the kiss morphed and became overpowering, insistent, and exhilarating. His tongue dominated hers, tangling and dancing with it at will. His hand tangled in her hair, fisting a hank of it and tugging her head back to expose her throat. Trapped. She had thought to be the aggressor, but there was no denying who was dominating who.

Fletch's kiss wasn't merely a kiss. It wasn't a prelude to anything else—it was complete in and of itself. She could feel his cock throbbing against her belly. When she tried to slide back to give it a little distance, Fletch had growled and used the hand not tangled in her hair to cup her ass and pull her close. She knew she should protest; knew things were getting out of control, but she just couldn't seem to find the wherewithal to do anything other than moan and give herself over to him.

His tongue slid between her lips and past her teeth, plundering her mouth to taste and explore. There was nothing tentative about the way he held her or made her surrender to him. This was no voyage of discovery, but a marauder invading a foreign territory to claim and conqueror.

"Fletch," she moaned.

"Claire," he replied as his hand slid up the inside

of her thigh and pushed her panties out of his way to stroke her labia before circling her clit.

"Oh, god," she said as her breathing became more shallow and erratic.

"At your service," he purred, his fingers sliding into her wet heat and stroking her rhythmically.

He held her close and kissed her deeply, swallowing her cry of ecstasy as her orgasm crashed all around her like a stormy night. Thunder rolled as lightning flashed and the car was illuminated. She could only hope the cabbie had his eyes on the road because if not, there would be no doubt in his mind as to what had just happened.

"I can't wait to get you in a proper bed," Fletch whispered along her throat.

The cabbie made the familiar turn into her driveway.

"Fletch…"

"One more word and I'll give the cabbie more to talk about than he already has."

The cab pulled up to her front door and Fletch fished around in his pocket and threw some bills at the driver. "Is that enough?"

"More than enough, sir, even with a generous tip," said the driver, getting out of the cab and opening their door.

"Keep the change and your mouth shut," replied Fletch as he stepped out of the car with Claire still basically in his lap.

He swung his arm under her legs and held her cradled to his chest. The night was raw and powerful —no rain, but plenty of wind, thunder, and lightning.

"You can depend on my discretion, sir. You and your lady have a very good evening."

He carried her to the door and let her lean down to key in the code that would unlock it. This was not good. Well, that wasn't true, this was very good, but he couldn't be here. If he discovered the high-end safe concealed in the hidden compartment in an antique desk, he might wonder why it was there.

And he sure as hell couldn't get in her bed. When she'd come home this afternoon to take a shower and change in order to meet him for dinner, she'd had no intention of sleeping with Fletch. That might not be precisely true, but she sure as hell hadn't planned for him to be here. While the desk safe was secure, it was a pain in the ass to get into, so she'd simply slipped the necklace into the zippered pillow protector and then into the pillowcase. It should be safe, but to be certain, she would have to ensure it was her head that rested on it.

Their dinner conversation had been provocative, and she wondered how much he knew. She doubted he could prove anything, but figured Mia's idea to lay low for a while might not be the worst thing. As he set her down, she realized all of the buttons down the front of her dress had been unfastened. He slid the dress and her bra off her shoulders, letting them fall to the floor in a puddle. He tipped her onto the bed, so she was on her back with her ass right at the edge with her legs hanging off.

It was a tall bed that she normally used a small stepstool to climb into. Claire realized as she looked up at him towering over her, that it was precisely the right height for him to fuck her with ease. Fletch knelt down and untied her gladiator sandals, removing them before he did the same with her panties.

"You are the most maddeningly beautiful woman who's ever graced the earth. You make me believe up is down and wrong is right. It might take me forever to forgive you for making me want you the way I do."

"What happens if you do?" she asked.

"I'll fuck you so hard you'll have trouble walking."

"And if you don't?"

The grin on his face became purely feral, "In that case, I'll spank your ass until you can't sit for a week, and then I'll fuck you just as hard. Spread your legs for me, Claire, and let me see your pussy."

Provocatively, she spread her legs, watching his face as the planes that formed it hardened with determination. He reached for the top button of his fly, and she sat up to help him. He pushed her back down and stepped between her legs, lifting her by the backs of her thighs as his enormous cock practically burst through his now open fly.

Holding her steady, he slowly impaled her with his cock pushing forward in the same incremental degrees that he pulled her to him. It was exquisite and nearly more than she could stand. Claire's body bowed and she cried out as Fletch filled her completely and then some. She had no idea her pussy could accommodate something that big. He groaned as he sank to his balls before pulling back and driving forward again. His eyes were riveted to where their bodies ebbed and flowed together. He was getting off on watching his cock fuck her; she was getting off on watching him watch.

Thunder provided the deep rhythm with which he thrust into her, and lightning lit up the bedroom so there was no place to hide. He pounded into her, claiming her as his. There was no doubt in either of their minds that this was no mere coming together to meet a mutual, physical need; no, this was Fletch staking his claim and believing she was surrendering to him.

His breath was ragged and drawn as he focused on her pleasure, driving up into her to hit that magic spot and making her pussy tremble and her body shake as she fell into an abyss of ecstasy where time and space, wrong and right no longer existed. There was only her and Fletch and the way he made her feel. She called his name as she came again, and he ground against her with a strangled groan as he poured himself into her.

"Now that that's out of the way, we can get onto the more serious task of the night," he said as he lifted her up, turned back the covers and set her down in the middle of the bed.

Claire scooched a little to one side, ensuring the pillow with the Grenadine Necklace was securely under her head. If he planned to fuck her into oblivion in order to search her place, he was welcome to do it. He'd never find the safe in the desk and she doubted very much he would search the pillow on which her head was laying.

"And what might that be?" she asked.

"Seeing just how many times I can make you come."

"Don't make promises you can't keep," she teased.

Fletch crawled onto the bed to kneel between her thighs and reached down to play with her nipples that were already responding to his presence. He leaned down and sucked her nipple into his mouth, swirling his tongue around it before giving it the edge of his teeth and making her hiss.

Claire ran her fingers through his thick dark hair. He was the most beautiful man she'd ever seen—all hard lines and muscles. His torso as he reared up and removed his sweater revealed a cut chest and washboard abs. His jeans had slid down to ride low on his hips, revealing those sexy hip notches and his cock that was getting stiffer.

Every time she tried to make him go faster, he slowed down, worshiping her body in a way no man ever had. She reveled in his adoration and lust, letting both flow over and around her as she savored each caress.

"It should be illegal for you to be this beautiful."

She didn't know if it was just a line, and she didn't care. For this one night she was going to believe it. All the times she'd been compared to Evangeline and other stunning women melted away. The only thing that mattered was that Fletch seemed to believe it, and he made her believe.

Fletch moved to the edge of the bed and instinctively she reached for him.

He leaned back over her. "I'm not going anywhere. I just want to get out of these boots and jeans."

Once he'd stripped himself naked, he rejoined her in bed and stretched out along her body, whispering in her ear all the ways he was going to fuck her, all the while his cock rubbed against her as his fingers played inside her. By the time he made a place for himself between her legs, she was aching and shaking with need.

Wrapping her arms around him, she welcomed his weight as he recaptured her mouth, thrusting inside to duel with hers. His cock throbbed against her clit, and she tried to move in a way that would force him to take her. Slipping his hands beneath her, he grasped the globes of her ass to hold her steady as he moved up inside her, using gentle shallow thrusts as her pussy softened to take him again.

"There's my girl," he crooned as he began to stroke more deeply and powerfully.

He was easily the most well-endowed man she'd ever been with, and at times the thrusting bordered on painful, but she pushed those thoughts away, focusing on the man himself and the lovely buzz that swirled all around her as her body began to build towards another orgasm. Claire reached around him to grab his ass, urging him to thrust harder and deeper. She tried to move with and against him, but he held her steady. The message was clear: she would take what he gave her and surrender her will to his.

Faster, deeper, and harder he pounded into her, making her climax again and again. Claire knew she was going to feel this come morning. He hadn't been kidding about robbing her of her ability to walk, but still, she could find no way to resist his possession. Finally, he gave a last, brutal thrust as all his muscles seized and he groaned into her ear as her pussy clamped down, milking his cock as he spilled his seed into her.

He allowed himself to rest on her as she sank into the mattress. When his breathing had returned to normal, he kissed her gently and then rolled to her side. As much as she wanted to cuddle against him, she had the presence of mind to know she needed to keep the pillow and what it contained firmly in her control. Scrunching it up, she placed her head on it towards the side closest to him and grasped the open end with her hands. She wasn't foolish enough to think he couldn't wrestle it away, but he'd have to wake her up in the process.

Not seeming to take any offense that she had turned away from him, he spooned against her, wrapping his arm around her. "There now," he rumbled, "that should teach you to doubt my veracity or my ability to take care of you in all ways."

A small warning flag went up—what the hell did he mean by that? And then the warning flags and everything else disappeared as Fletch wove a sensual web around her throughout the night, repeatedly making love to her in ways that went beyond mere physical pleasure. She could feel her soul yearning to join with him. Being with him, having him in her bed blocked out everything but arousal, need, and satisfaction in what seemed to be an endless circle.

Sometime before dawn, Fletch rolled off the bed, pulled on his jeans and began to methodically search the mill house. He was thorough and quiet, she'd give him that. She watched him through hooded eyes with a mixture of interest, amusement and outrage with a tinge of sadness. The sadness came both from wondering if the sex had been just a ruse and knowing they could never be. But never once did he even come close to finding the hidden safe or the treasure on which she rested her weary head.

As the sun finally began to emerge in the east, Claire heard him head out of the house and down to the barn. She slipped out of bed, groaning as the ache in her sex made itself known. Gingerly, she moved to the window and watched as he went toward the barn. He stopped long enough to pull on his cowboy boots and sweater, which was a damn shame as she wouldn't have minded getting to watch him move without his shirt on, his muscles rippling in the morning light. He fed and watered the horses, ensuring their silent cooperation, and began to search the barn. Finding nothing, he mucked out their stalls. He must be feeling at least a little bit guilty—most likely more from searching her home than how he'd ravaged her body repeatedly throughout the night.

As far as Claire was concerned, he needn't have felt guilty about either. She heard a vehicle on the drive and saw an unfamiliar car pull up. Unknown to her, but apparently not to him. He slipped into the passenger side front seat and closed the door behind him as the car pulled away. As she walked back to the bed, she spotted a note he must have written:

Claire,

Last night was amazing. I'll call you later.

Sleep as much as you can. I'll feed, water, and muck the stalls before I go.

We need to talk. I think we need to clear the air between us.

Fletch

She crawled back into bed, snuggling into the covers and cuddling her treasure-hiding pillow close. He could talk until he was blue in the face. She'd made a promise to Poppi and as the poem said, she had miles to go before she slept. She yawned.

Although maybe a few more hours of sleep wouldn't hurt.

CHAPTER 12

CLAIRE

The second time she woke, the sun was high in the sky. Claire stretched, hoping some of the ache would be gone, but no such luck. She had to give him credit, he'd been as good as his word. There were few parts of her body that didn't feel the excess from the night before. She stepped into her shower, glad once again that she had opted to spend for the steam option.

Claire leaned her head against the tile, letting the water cascade over her body as the steam opened up her pores and let the excesses of the night before seep out. The water felt good as she closed her eyes and remembered the way his big, callused hands had felt on her skin as he played her body like Yo-Yo Ma played the cello. And her body responded in the same way by making sweet and haunting music.

She could easily recall his hands cupping her

breasts, fingers tugging and pinching her nipples and clit before soothing the ache with his mouth and tongue. God, the man knew how to kiss, how to caress and how to fuck. He was positively addictive. She knew she should have resisted him, found some way to refuse him when he'd pulled her beneath him for the umpteenth time, but she hadn't. Even this morning there was a sensual hum that flowed through her body —one she'd never felt before and might not ever feel again.

She toweled off her body, wrapping the towel around her hair and slathering on moisturizer before starting to pull on a pair of leggings and discovering the beard burn he'd left on the sensitive flesh at the top of her thighs and just above her sex. Instead, she opted for comfy pajama pants and a soft cashmere, slouchy sweater that she'd found at a vintage clothing store. Normally in the mornings she was up with the sun and trotting down the stairs. Fletch seeing to her horses' needs had allowed her to sleep in.

Removing the necklace from its temporary hiding place, she started to move down her stairs with her usual spring in her step, but her body said, 'No. Just no.' It had a point. She probably shouldn't have tried to make up for all the sex she hadn't had in a very long time all in one night. Once downstairs, despite the protests of her body that it needed coffee, she slipped the Grenadine Necklace in the safe in the hidden compartment of the desk that looked out over her pasture.

Claire brewed a large mug of coffee, adding a large dollop of heavy cream before walking to her kitchen table and sitting down. She considered getting up and making breakfast, but that sounded like an awful lot of trouble, even though she knew she should feed her body, especially after last night's excesses. How was it that he had seemed to move easily and without any residual stiffness or discomfort? Although, she supposed, he was the one with the battering ram between his legs and she was the one he'd used it on, but dear, god had it felt fantastic.

Getting involved with Fletch, even seeing him again, was dangerous. She was certain he knew she was the thief behind the heists. He hadn't worked out all the pieces yet, and didn't know how to prove it, but she knew he would be relentless in his pursuit of bringing her to justice. But still he called to her in a way no man had done before, and she was beginning to want to answer that call, regardless of the consequences.

As she'd done so many times since he'd passed, she wished Poppi was here for her to talk to. He had raised her to be open and forthright with him about her feelings, needs, and desires. Many a night they'd sat up in front of the fire, drinking tea with honey until the sun came up. She couldn't drink hot tea with honey anymore; it reminded her too much of him and ripped the scar of her grief open so that it would weep once more.

What would he have thought of Fletch? She was certain as a man he would have liked him. The way he'd made love to her, she knew he had to be able to ride a horse with the best of them. To Claire, there was little that was as sexy as a man who could handle a horse with sensitivity and strength, making the horse their partner in whatever endeavor they were undertaking.

But Poppi would caution her to decide what was truly important to her before spending any more time with Fletch. She had long ago been able to return the jewelry he had stolen to those to whom it truly belonged. The insurance company had paid out millions—thus the size of the bounty on her head—but they'd also raked in all those insurance premiums over the years, and those from whom Poppi had stolen had been paid by the insurance company. It was a balancing of the scales she could justify and live with, but she very much doubted that Fletch would see it the same way.

Once she'd restored the jewelry Poppi had stolen, she'd begun to research, find, and recover other pieces. What had started out as a sacred duty to honor her grandfather had become something of a lark, which in turn had become her own holy grail.

Until now, no one had ever guessed that she even knew about the thefts, much less had been the one who perpetrated them. And while Fletch might *know*, there wasn't a damn thing he could *prove*. Understanding her own weakness, she vowed to avoid Fletch at all costs. It would be far too easy to give into the temptation he offered to walk the straight and narrow line.

Claire heard another vehicle coming up her drive. Glancing at the clock, she grinned. Mia, as always, was right on time. She got up and put a pod of Mia's favorite coffee in her Keurig drizzling honey into the mug to have it at the ready as Mia came through the door.

"Have you lost your fucking mind? Oh no, that's it. You lost your mind fucking a man who is trying to collect the bounty on your head."

"Good morning to you, too," said Claire as she sat back down in the kitchen chair, "and yes, I had a lovely time fucking the delectable Mr. Fletcher. Thanks so much for asking. Apparently, I was more out of practice than I thought, not because he had any complaints but because I don't think there's enough ibuprofen in the world to take away all my aches and pains. But it was so much fun getting them."

"Seriously, Claire. I'm glad you had a good time, but he's got his people doing a deep dive on you."

"I thought you'd scrubbed anything that might point a finger at us."

"I did, too. What I wasn't counting on was Carter Hall."

"Hawkman from *Legends of Tomorrow?*"

"What? Oh no, Carter Hall is the name of Fletcher's IT guy. Genius out of MIT. Graduated at like twelve. Devoted to Fletcher. He's the one who's been attacking our firewalls. Somehow, he got hold of Seamus O'Donnell's prison record…"

"Shit. That led him to being my guardian and Poppi working for Sir Godfrey."

"Do you think they know about Sir Godfrey's father and all the crap he got up to with the Nazis?"

"In all honesty, I don't think the man collaborated with the Nazis. I do think he scooped up jewelry taken from their victims, but still, I suppose that is only one step removed from working with those goose-stepping bastards."

"Is the necklace in the safe?" Mia asked. She always worried until she knew whatever they had stolen was in the safe, or better yet, in the hands of those to whom it truly belonged.

"It is, although it spent the night in my pillowcase…"

"What?" Mia squeaked.

"I didn't have time to get it into the safe, so I hid it in my pillowcase. I wasn't really planning on spending the night with Fletch, and if I did, I thought we'd be at the Savoy, but things changed, and we ended up here." Claire laughed. "He searched the millhouse and barn this morning when he thought I was asleep. Although, gentleman that he is, he did feed my horses and muck out their stalls." She shook her head. "He never knew how close he was to that necklace. But it's in the safe now."

"When is it leaving?"

"Just as soon as our contact can make the connections and get here. I would say it'll be gone before the end of the week."

Mia got up and started pacing, taking sips of her coffee as she did so. "I'm telling you; this has to be the last one for a while. Things are heating up all over."

"But if we quit now, won't they figure out it's us?"

"I think that we're past that stage, and what's worse, I don't think Fletcher and his group are the only ones who know."

"Why do you say that?" asked Claire, knowing that it took a lot to spook Mia.

"I had an anonymous—and I do mean anonymous—note from someone who broke into our secure chatroom on the dark web."

"How could that happen?"

"I don't know. Those firewalls and protocols are bulletproof or at least they should have been. The only way in was through one of our couriers."

"Hawkman?"

Mia laughed. "I wish, but no. I checked out his systems—personal, the one he keeps for Fletch himself, and the one for Silver Arrow Security. I couldn't break in, but I could get far enough to tell it wasn't him. I don't have a clue who it is. I tried to shut down the chatroom, but I've been locked out of any of the administrative stuff. I can access it like anyone who has the passwords, but I no longer have any control."

"How could somebody lock us out of our own chatroom?"

"I don't know, Claire. If I thought it was Carter, I would just assume he was working under Fletch's orders. But it isn't him. I'm sure of it."

"What is it, Mia? What has you so afraid?"

"They didn't just get into the chatroom and shut me out, they left a message, and they left it where anyone who had access to the chatroom can see it."

"If the message is to me, why would they leave it for anyone to see?"

"My guess is, they want to frighten everyone—not just us, but anyone who's looking to do business with us."

Claire looked at her quizzically. "What did the message say?"

"It was a threat, Claire," said Mia, a shiver passing through her body.

"Mia, what did it say?"

"Basically, it said he or she knows who you are—but they didn't reveal your identity. They want us to give them the Grenadine Necklace…"

"Shit."

"Exactly…"

"So, whoever it is knows we have it and knows that even on the black market the necklace is worth more than the bounty on my head. A bounty we didn't know about until Fletch told me about it."

"I was thinking the same thing. Do you think it's Fletch?"

Claire shook her head. "I doubt it. I don't think he'd blackmail me, and he sure as hell wouldn't take stolen property. The only way he might even threaten to out me is if he was trying to get the necklace back, as his company was hired to protect it. Even if he was trying to save me from myself and break our network apart, I can't see him threatening me. I just can't see it being him."

"I agree. Fletcher seems like a pretty straight arrow. I just can't see him doing that, and for the record I can't see him trying to collect the bounty."

Claire nodded. "Agreed. I think if he thought it was somebody else, he'd be all over it, but I think there's something between us and I don't think he wants to harm me. It has to be either some scumbag at Lloyd's of London or one of the other insurance agencies—somebody who has access to that information."

"I'm scared, Claire. The note said they have evidence and if we don't pay, they'll out you and collect the ten million."

"So, not only has he threatened me, but he's also

let everyone else who had access to the chatroom know that there are ten million reasons to rat us out."

"But they don't know our names."

"But they've seen my face. No. I don't think any of our couriers would turn on us. Like us, they're true believers. Remember how we had to argue with them to let us even cover their expenses? No. I don't believe they'll turn. Someone else has somehow broken in and is looking for a big payday. Any chance it could be Fletch's IT guy?"

"Nah. He's a total geek; he was only a black hat hacker because he believed he was fighting the good fight. If anything, I think he'd want to help me. And the note said they have 'evidence,' but that could be a bluff. We have only one hundred, sixty-three hours and forty-three minutes until they blow up our world."

"How do you know that?"

Mia turned her laptop around so Claire could see the screen. Up in the left-hand corner of the screen was a bomb with a lit fuse showing the initial time given and next to it was a stopwatch counting down the time until the blackmailer would expose them. The time shown on the bomb remained constant while the stopwatch continued to count down the seconds, minutes and hours.

Tic-Tic-Tic

CHAPTER 13

CLAIRE

*S*he sat with Mia, sipping their coffee, contemplating what to do.

"There are just so many more people who without us will never be able to recover what was stolen from them," said Claire. "We need to find out who is behind this threat and if they have any real evidence. For all we know they simply have conjecture and suspicion. But maybe you should go to Aruba or the Amalfi Coast for a couple of months…"

"I'm not leaving you alone to deal with this," Mia said, interrupting her.

"I would not be alone. I could always appeal to Fletch's protective nature, throw myself at his feet and beg for mercy."

"You suck at begging."

Claire grinned. "True, but I got a lot better at it last night. Fletch responds positively to the word please." Mia rolled her eyes. "Besides, and more importantly, you would still be able to support me via the internet."

"I know you had a great time last night, but I do find it a bit suspicious that you steal the Grenadine Necklace—the only one his company had been hired to keep safe, and then we get the threat. I don't want to burst your bubble, but guys who look like Fletch don't usually date girls who look like us."

Mia had a point. Could Fletch have been playing her?

"I don't want to think that, but I also can't say positively that it isn't him."

"I don't think he has the skills…"

"But Carter does, and Carter works for him and seems pretty damn loyal. But then again, Fletch does believe in our cause, just thinks there are legal ways to do the job."

"But there aren't."

"I know, but he wants to believe that in the end, right will win the day. But we know he's wrong and that in the end, we'll be the ones who come out on the right side of history. I think it's more likely that he'd take me in for the bounty. Ten million dollars is a lot of money, and he did know about it."

Memories of the night before threatened to overwhelm her—the way he touched her, the way his kisses chased all her fears away, the way when he stroked into her nothing else seemed important.

"Look, Mia, I'm not going to lie to you. Fletch isn't the only one standing on the edge. What scares me the most is that I want to take his hand and jump in with him, but if I'm going to do that…"

"Would you? Could you walk away from everything we've done? Just call it a day and walk into whatever happily ever after looks like for you?"

"I'm not sure I couldn't. We've been doing this a long time. We've both given up huge chunks of our lives, taken huge risks, and forsaken most of those who were once close to us. Don't you think we deserve to have a happily ever after? Sometimes I wonder if we haven't paid whatever dues we owe ourselves or anyone else?"

"I know your granda didn't believe that."

"Maybe. Or maybe he just found a way to strike back at the men who got him tossed out of the army with a dishonorable discharge. And maybe he thought it was some kind of penance he had to pay for my parents' death."

"You were never his penance. He adored you. You were his world. I watched him watch you compete— saw him beam as you cleared every jump."

"He worked for a man he loathed in order to keep me with him and to give me the things he thought I should have, and each day it ate a tiny bit of his soul away. I know it was Sir Godfrey's father, but still, without his ill-gotten gains, he never could have dragged his noble, but impoverished, family out of the gutter so his son could have the best education and attract a wealthy wife."

Mia laid her hand on Claire's arm. "I don't think he regretted his decision. Seeing you shine—seeing you become the woman you are. I know he would make the same choices again. Are you sure about Fletch?"

Claire was quiet and then closed her eyes, taking a deep breath. "My heart wants to be, but my brain isn't convinced. And neither is he. He did search my place, right? Perhaps I should return the favor."

"Search his room at the Savoy?"

"No. That's his hotel room. His home is in Devon, at Albion Farm. It shouldn't be too hard to find."

"We don't really think he threatened you, do we?"

"I don't know, and that's what makes me think I should find out if he has anything. I'm so fucking confused. I can't see him actually sending me to prison, but I could see him making a threat to force my hand and either turn to him for help or walk away completely."

"Welcome to the reality the rest of us have to live with."

"What do you mean?"

"For as long as I've known you, you've had a clear vision of your path. At first it was to beat people like the Robbins at their own game so you could get your grandfather out of there. Then once you knew what he was doing, his cause became your own."

"I need answers, and I think some of them may well lie in Devon. Do you think you could head back to London and keep an eye on him for me?"

"Absolutely. In fact, let's make this a two-pronged attack."

"What are you thinking?"

Mia pulled out two small electronic recording devices. "What do you say you go to Devon, search the place and then plant a bug. I'll do the same in his hotel room."

"That sounds like a plan. Do you still have that cell phone tracker app you put on our phones?" Mia nodded. "Good. That way the first chance I have to get to his phone, I can download it onto his. He won't know or be able to track it back to us, right?"

"Yes. It's the same one a lot of parents use to keep an eye on their kids. All you have to do is open the app on your phone, get it within a foot to eighteen inches of his phone, and hit install on the app's menu. It takes about fifteen seconds to do. Keep in mind if he's got Carter working for him, he may be sweeping his room at the Savoy. These little beauties," Mia said, holding up the bugs, "are my own design. They have a limited jamming capability that will make them more difficult to detect. I'm not saying Carter wouldn't find them if he was looking for them, but they might pass a general sweep."

"Anything to tie it back to us?"

"None."

"Then we have little to lose and everything to gain."

After Mia left, Claire settled down to see if she could find an address for Fletch's farm in Devon. Surprisingly, she entered 'Albion Farm'—the guy really did have a thing for Robin Hood—and sure enough, he had a website, which listed the farm's address. She needed to dress the part of a prospective buyer. If he caught her, there would be no explanation but some variation of the truth, but if she was seen casually by someone just driving by, she needed to be wearing breeches and boots. If anyone other than Fletch confronted her about being there, she could present herself as a prospective buyer and say she was looking for him. She groaned, breeches hugging her chafed thighs did not sound comfortable, but this might be her only chance to take a look around his farm.

Claire went back to her bedroom, relinquishing the comfy pajama pants in favor of a pair of breeches. She pulled on riding boots and opted to wear the cashmere sweater she'd had on earlier. Grabbing a travel mug of coffee, she headed out to her garage, which had once been part of the original mill structure. She had three vehicles to choose from—her vintage Triumph Spitfire, her reliable lorry with which she pulled her horse trailer, and her Range Rover. The Spitfire was the most fun as it was a convertible, and it was a gorgeous day, but inconspicuous it was not. The lorry was the most in keeping with her 'cover' as a prospective buyer. The Range Rover was actually the most comfortable, the most practical and could be appropriate for someone coming to look at Fletch's horses. *Range Rover it is!*

After checking the petrol and opening the panoramic sunroof, she headed west out of Greenwich toward Devon. It was an almost four-hour drive —too long to listen to her own thoughts; better to listen to music and sing along. The time passed quickly as the drive itself was beautiful, and Claire loved to drive. The two places she did her best thinking were driving one of her vehicles or riding one of her horses. She queued up her Pandora playlist for 'driving songs,' and closed in on her target. One thing she had learned to do while casing various homes and museums was to blend in. Hopefully that wouldn't come into play today, but it was a good tool to have in her arsenal.

Naturally, Fletch's property had to be in the northwest corner of Devon, but she could immediately see what had attracted him to it. Albion Farm was a glorious piece of property, with rolling, lush pastures located on the headland above what appeared to be a private beach. Driving past the entrance to his farm, she looked for a place to park the Range Rover where it couldn't be easily seen. She followed a dirt track that headed toward the beach and realized she'd found the spot where the local teens came to party and hang out. She planned to be gone long before any of them should show up. Locking the Range Rover, she began to make her way back along the beach to Fletcher's home.

There was a winding path that led from the headlands down to the beach itself. There was plenty of evidence that he worked his horses down on the beach. She loved seeing the small hoofprints which had to be from foals running alongside their mothers. Claire began walking up the path, noting the place he had planted native flora. The overall effect was lovely, and she inhaled the sea air deeply. Living on the Thames was wonderful, but it didn't compare to living at the beach.

As she reached the top of the path, she got her first good look at Fletch's home, which was impressive, made of stone and had a commanding view of both the beach and his pastures. He'd opted for rustic stone and natural wood fencing. The pastures all had lovely lean-tos that seemed to fit in with the feel of the place. The horses looked well-cared for and happy. She followed the path up to the back of the house, where she found a brick patio and a door leading into what she suspected was the kitchen. So not only was it pretty, but it was also practical. In many ways, it reminded her of the man himself.

The good thing about being a jewel thief was that early on you learned how to spot and get around alarm systems. She approached his back door, put on a pair of gloves before disengaging the alarm and letting herself in, resetting the alarm after she did so.

Turning around, she tried to orient herself in the house. The house had been extensively remodeled. The kitchen was enormous and boasted open upper shelves with live edges, sage green cabinets below, an island and beautiful stone countertops that complemented the colors within the house which reflected its beachy vibe.

Perhaps there would be a time in the future she could actually take a tour of the house with Fletch and discuss it. It seemed to capture all of its old-world charm with a lot of modern comforts. But exploring those would have to wait, as well.

Claire crossed the room to a niche where Fletch had situated an elegant vintage desk. Most of the electronics were hidden and she began to probe to see what she could find. He had an external hard drive, which she downloaded onto the thumb drive Mia had given her. As she was copying the information, she rifled through the papers on his desk, being careful to put them in the same precise spot. She also looked through his files, finding one labeled 'Grenadine' and one 'Master Thief.' It seemed Fletch had been tracking the pattern of her and Poppi's thefts long before now. Using her cell phone, she took pictures of each piece of paper in the two files and then a picture of the files all in a row in each of the drawers.

Once the download was complete, Claire began to

move around the main room, which looked out over the pastures and barn. She delicately poked and prodded pieces of the decorative trim surrounding the mantel, looking for some kind of fingerhold, trigger or button that when activated would reveal a safe, hidey hole, or something that might lead to some kind of secret stash. She felt like a bit of a snoop, but if whoever it was that had threatened them wasn't bluffing, they could spend a good portion of the rest of their lives in prison.

Methodically, she began to move around the room. Two bookcases flanked the fireplace, but had been skillfully designed to hold books, various knick-knacks and framed pictures. The overall look was esthetically pleasing but it would take hours to fully search them.

She trotted up the steps to the upper level, noting a definite creak in the third step from the top. To the right were two bedrooms with a jack and jill bath between them. To the left, toward the beach side was the primary bedroom and bath. There was a large walk-in closet as well as a stacked laundry. The fact that they were navy blue as opposed to white, black or stainless steel for some reason pleased her more than it should. She was willing to bet there was a commercial grade laundry out in the barn for horse blankets, towels, and the like.

Once again, she moved around the walk-in closet, using her fingers to probe the shelving units to find any spaces that might be hidden. She grinned as she felt a kind of latch tucked beneath the molding on one of the shelves. Pressing it, she was gratified to feel a click as the shelf swiveled on some sort of hidden axis to open. She was just about to access the area when she heard the creak of the third step from the top.

Shit! Someone was here and about to find her. Claire thought about hiding in whatever was behind the shelf, but there was no way to know how deep it was. She could remain in the closet, but if it was Fletch, the closet and bath were probably the first place he would head. She ran out, grateful Poppi had taught her to move quickly and quietly, to slide under the bed, but realized there was no bed skirt to conceal her presence.

The footsteps in the hall were coming closer. There really was no place to hide. That wasn't necessarily true. The enormous bed was flanked on either side by French doors which led out onto the balcony. If she could get out onto it, she could most likely climb down. After all it was a house made of stone, which meant natural hand and foot holds.

The footsteps were getting louder. Not enough time to get out on the balcony and hide. There were heavy damask curtains that could be pulled across the French doors in order to block out the sunlight. Trite and cliché it might be, but it would have to do.

Heart thumping, she dove behind the curtains.

CHAPTER 14

CLAIRE

The footsteps hesitated just outside the door. She'd been careful to return the slightly ajar door to its original position. Had she miscalculated? Had he noticed? The door was pushed in, allowing whoever it was to enter just as she ducked behind the drapes, hoping like hell her black boots weren't peeking out from underneath the curtains.

She heard a familiar groan; one she'd heard a number of nights before. Claire could feel her body come alive in response to his proximity—her nipples became stiff, and her pussy clenched and then softened, readying itself for his use and pleasure. *Good lord; I'm as pathetic as a teenage girl after her first orgasm.*

She peeked out from behind the curtains and watched as he moved around the room, tossing his shirt into a hamper in the closet and allowing her a glimpse of his muscular physique. There were tattoos and scars all over his body that she wanted the time to explore with her fingers and tongue. He really was the most gloriously made man she'd ever seen.

Sitting on the edge of the opposite side of the bed from her, Fletch set his phone, wallet, and keys on the nightside table, pulling off his boots before removing his jeans and briefs. Fletch looked really hot in clothes. Claire had noticed the admiring glances from other restaurant patrons the night before. But if he was hot when clothed, he was smoking hot when he was naked. His back and ass were magnificent pieces of work and had felt splendid under her fingers last night as he'd plowed into her over and over again.

Fletch tossed the rest of his clothes in the hamper and put his boots on the shoe rack before moving into the primary bath. The shower started up and she heard him step in. She ran around to the other side of the bed and initiated the app to install the electronic tracker in his phone.

Pleased with herself and her plan to go out the set of French doors on this side and escape down the roof, she had to bite her lip to keep from shrieking when his cell rang and vibrated in her hand. She glanced at the door to the bath, relieved to see he wasn't one of those people who were so afraid of missing out on something that they answered every phone call, message, or text. She glanced at the caller ID: Emil Franklin. Who the hell was Emil Franklin and why was his name so familiar?

Emil Franklin. Emil Franklin. Emil Franklin, she repeated, trying to get it ingrained in her mind. Why did that name ring a bell? Maybe she'd seen it downstairs in the paperwork she'd photographed. She'd need to check as soon as she was safely away.

The sound of the shower being cut off caught her attention. Quickly, she set the phone back in its place and slipped out the French doors, moving toward the edge of the balcony furthest away from the bath, keeping herself concealed as she looked for a way down.

She saw him glance at his phone before tossing it back down and moving away from the bed, back to the bathroom. Once he was safely back in the bath, Claire peered over the side of the railing, happy to see that she had been correct in her assessment of the house's scalability. Swinging a leg over the side of the railing, she found a good path of hand and footholds and swung out onto the side of the wall. The trick to climbing down a wall or cliff made of stone was to move slowly and steadily. Moving hand over hand and foot by foot, she gradually made her way to the ground. It might have been quicker to go straight down, but she moved diagonally so that she ended up being at ground level on the side of the building. That would give her good cover as she ran back down to the beach and made her way back to her vehicle. She would be exposed but less so than if she tried to cross his pastures or just walked up the road.

After leaving his beach without being spotted and making her way back to her Range Rover, she called Mia.

"Are you okay? He didn't see you?" asked Mia in a frightened voice.

"I'm fine. I am a master jewel thief, after all. Breaking into his house wasn't all that hard. You'd have thought a guy with his own security team would have, well, better security. I managed to download his external hard drive and took a lot of photos of two files. Do we know anyone named Emil Franklin?"

"The name doesn't sound familiar, but I'll start tracking him down. Shit! Where are you?"

"A little bit north and east of his place, why?"

"Thank god, then, he's not after you. His phone shows him as being on the move. Did you have a chance to download the whole app?"

"I did…"

"Goodie. That means we can tap into his phone calls. He's making one now. It's to an unknown caller. Shall I patch you in?"

"Absolutely. If it's anything I'll let you know and you can send me his location."

"Gotcha. Stay safe. That damn stopwatch in the chatroom is still ticking away."

There was some static and then she could hear the narrative as clear as day. Claire muted her own phone to ensure the others wouldn't know she was listening in. Her caller ID showed her that Fletch was on one end of the conversation, but the other party was not identified.

"I'm pretty damn sure I know who took the necklace," said Fletch.

"I demand you tell me who," snarled the male voice on the other end of the line. The voice sounded older and not British, French, or German—perhaps Dutch, Austrian, or Swiss?

"I'm not telling you anything until I can prove my suspicions, and even then, we're going to do this legally. I will work with the authorities to apprehend the suspect."

"You will bring this thief to me."

"That's not happening."

"I hired you to catch this thief…"

"No. You hired me to protect your necklace, and when my best efforts failed to do that, I offered to try and retrieve your necklace and return it to you. At no time did I tell you I would turn anyone over to you or condone you exacting any kind of revenge on whoever it was."

"It is not revenge. It is justice. They took what is mine."

"And when I return it to you, it will be yours again. If that doesn't suit you, then I will simply turn all my findings over to the authorities, and you can file an insurance claim."

"You will regret working for me, Fletcher."

"I already do, but if you think you're going to make a move on me or my people, you'd best think again. I tend to react badly to people who make threats against those I care about and even worse if someone actually tries to harm them. My team is all

former special forces. You don't want to go up against us. You'll lose."

There was silence on the other end.

"Do we understand each other?" asked Fletch.

"We understand one another, but you should understand, I make a better friend than an enemy."

"I'm on my way to a meeting with the Yard. They will be preparing the search warrant we need to search the suspect's home and make an arrest."

It occurred to Claire that Fletch was being very careful not only about not naming her, but not indicating in any way, shape, or form that she was female. Who was this mysterious caller? Why was Fletch being so evasive? Did he truly believe the caller might be a threat to her and Mia?

The call ended, and Claire had a feeling that neither party had been especially happy with the way the call ended. She was, however, feeling happy and relaxed. If Fletch was being honest with his mystery caller—perhaps the mysterious Emil Franklin?—then he was headed to the Yard. But why would Fletch be returning the Grenadine Necklace to him? The insurance claim for the theft had been filed by the descendants of the Petacci family. She made a mental note to check, but she didn't think Emil Franklin was among them.

She called Mia. "So, that was interesting."

"Why do you say that?" asked Mia.

"I don't know who the other caller was, but the

conversation got a bit heated. Fletch let the guy know that he knew who the thief was but couldn't prove it. He indicated he would reacquire the necklace, but he would not turn the thief over to whoever it was. He took great care not to indicate the gender of the thief."

"He's protecting you."

"Yes, but the question remains, why?"

"Did it ever occur to you that he might have feelings for you?"

"Yes, but it doesn't matter. He's never going to condone or understand what it is we do, and there are too many things left undone. I promised Poppi…"

"Who would have told you to quit if someone was threatening you or if there was someone in your life with whom you could build a future."

Claire knew Mia spoke the truth, but she wasn't ready to give it up. If she was being honest, it wasn't only about righting old wrongs; she was a bit of an adrenaline junkie and beating the system time and again was a real high. But for the first time she questioned what she wanted to do with her life. Her path had always seemed so clear and Fletch had caused her to question everything.

"That may be, but I'm not ready to quit. I need you to do two things for me. First, see if you can backtrace that call and find out who Fletch was talking to. And second, see if there's a search warrant being readied to be served on me."

"Do you think they'll find something?"

"No. I have no doubt the safe will stay hidden, as will everything I use to pull off the jobs. What I want to know is whether Fletch is really working with the Yard to apprehend the thief, or is that just something he told the other guy to help back him off?"

"What happens if they show up at your place in Greenwich?"

"I'll let them in and offer them a cup of coffee."

Mia laughed. "You're bad. You are very bad."

"Yes, I am, and I'm so good at it."

"How about if I swing by and take you out to my place for the weekend. We can make fresh pizza dough and build our own pizzas. We can kick back, eat pizza, have a beer, and watch a movie."

"Sounds like a plan. I'll get ready now. Just honk when you're out front. I'll come down."

Claire got back on the main road, cranked up Bon Jovi, and headed into London. She didn't notice the black sedan that moved off the shoulder of the road and remained two cars behind her until it was almost too late to do anything about it.

CHAPTER 15

CLAIRE

*L*ike a lot of women, Claire had been taught to watch for a tail, especially one that might be later in the day when she could be headed for home. The black sedan got a little lazy in the heavy London traffic and moved right up behind her. The first two turns made her notice it, as she tended to take a circuitous path to Mia, never wanting to lead trouble to her friend's door. When she made a deliberate, last-minute turn into an obscure alley and the car followed, she knew just what to do. Claire drove in a very deliberate manner to the Victoria Embankment—the home of Scotland Yard. As she pulled up, she hailed a bobby who pointedly looked at the sedan as it pulled past her and quickly lost itself in the morass of London's rush hour.

"Thank you, officer," she said pleasantly.

He tipped his hat. "My pleasure, ma'am. Would you like an escort home?"

"No but thank you. I have a few errands to run."

She didn't, but he didn't need to know that. Poppi had never been one to volunteer information to law enforcement and he'd taught her to do the same. Claire drove around for another twenty minutes, circling back and using roundabouts to ensure she hadn't picked up another tail. Pulling up in front of Mia's she honked. Mia must have been waiting just inside as she was out and in the car in nothing flat.

"We're going to take a little ride in the other direction from my place and then head to Greenwich on the back roads," Claire said as Mia hopped inside.

"Trouble?" Mia asked looking around.

"I picked up a tail just outside London. I took them to the Yard. A very nice bobby came out to help me. The driver of the black sedan did not look amused."

Mia laughed and they meandered their way back to Claire's millhouse, stopping at two different grocers as well as a petrol station. Once they were at the millhouse, they parked in the garage, set the alarm, and then took the tunnel from it to the main house. Claire had discovered both the tunnel and a bolt hole during the renovation project and had opted to make them stable and had then bribed her contractor and architect to keep their existence off the official blueprints filed with the city.

"I love that you have a secret entrance and way to get from the house to the garage," said Mia. "Do we need to worry about the horses?"

"No. I asked my neighbor to feed them on my way out of town, and yes, the tunnel has proved useful a time or two. I didn't see anyone following us…"

"Nor did I."

"But I figured better safe than sorry," Claire said, keying in the access code for the alarm system as she tripped the hidden latch from inside the bolt hole and let them into the main house. She closed the hidden access door and then re-armed the alarm.

"Snug as a couple of bugs in a rug," said Mia with a mischievous smile. "What did you have in mind for our viewing pleasure?"

"I thought perhaps an Alfred Hitchcock double feature—Cary Grant in *North by Northwest* and Jimmy Stewart in *Rear Window.*"

Claire set out the ingredients for her quick pizza dough and made a double batch. "The dough is made. What's your pleasure?"

"I want that four cheese one you make."

"Ah, the *Quattro Formaggi.*" Claire opened the fridge with a flourish. "Let me see what I've got in the way of cheese. Oooh, you're in luck—chevre, gorgonzola, ricotta salata, mozzarella, and roasted garlic on a garlic/olive oil base. An excellent choice."

"What are you having?" Mia asked laughing.

"I think I'll make a *Genovese* with fresh spinach,

sun-dried tomatoes, feta and roasted garlic and peppers on a walnut pesto base."

"Oh, I love that one, too."

"I tell you what, how about we do one of each and we split them?"

"Perfection. Want me to make salad while you make the pizzas?"

"And ruin a perfectly good beer and pizza night? Heaven forbid. Why don't you go settle yourself in the spare room while I get these made and in the oven?"

"Sounds good."

After placing the pizzas in to bake, Claire ran up to her own room, stripped out of her clothes and into a comfortable, stretchy knit maxi dress. She padded back down into the kitchen in her bare feet.

Mia had just rejoined her when the pizzas were coming out of the oven. "Yum. Those smell delicious."

"It's the roasted garlic. Come on, let's go get comfortable."

"I went through your DVDs and grabbed the movies. I queued up *Rear Window*."

They had just settled in on the chesterfield sofa when there was a hard knock on the door.

"What the hell?" said Claire.

The proximity alarm that should have gone off had remained silent. She picked up her double-barreled shotgun from the antique gun case and loaded it. Mia was in place to open the door so that it was between her and whoever was knocking. Claire looked down at her cell phone. Shit! It was Fletch and his techie, Carter.

Claire nodded and Mia flung open the door so that Fletch was confronted by a loaded shotgun being leveled at him by Claire. She needed him to understand she meant business and that she wasn't just going to roll over for him.

Fletch stepped back. "Fuck, Claire. What the hell is wrong with you?" he snarled as he stepped forward and shoved the barrel of the gun up so even if she'd pulled the trigger all that would have happened is she'd have damaged one of the beams in her ceiling before he disarmed her. "You could have hurt somebody."

"That was my intention. How the hell did you get past my proximity alarm?"

"That thing? Child's play to Carter. Mia, come out from behind the door."

Mia peeked around the door. "How do you know my name, and that I was here?"

"You don't really suppose my team and I are so inept that we don't know exactly who you are, do you? My guess is you know Carter."

"Only by reputation," said Mia, blushing.

Claire rolled her eyes. "Give me back my shotgun."

"No," said Fletch as he broke open the shotgun and removed the ammunition. "Carter, take my keys and get Mia out of here. Take her to the safehouse and keep her secure. There should be a team there already."

Claire tried to snatch the shotgun from Fletch, who merely slapped her hand. "That hurt."

"I told you no."

"You're not the boss of me," Claire snarled.

Handing the shotgun to Carter, he hauled Claire into his arms, his hand fisting her hair as he gripped the back of her neck and his arm snaked around her waist, holding her close. His mouth hovered over hers as he said very softly and distinctly, "You are the single most infuriating woman I've ever known and for reasons that escape me, I'm crazy about you."

His lips came down on hers in a fiery kiss that left Claire shaking in his arms as she grasped his muscular biceps and held on.

"Well, I'll just take Ms. Kelly…" said Carter.

"Mia is fine."

Carter grinned at her. He was actually rather handsome in a muscular nerd kind of way. "I'll just take Mia and leave you two alone to figure this out." He proffered his arm to Mia. "May I?"

"Sure. But could we grab one of the pizzas? I'm starving."

"You betcha." Carter nipped past Claire and Fletch as Fletch pressed Claire into the wall. Carter grabbed a pizza, and then escorted Mia out to Fletch's SUV.

Claire barely registered when they left, as their departure was covered by Fletch slamming the door behind them and then locking it. His tongue played along the seam of her lips, demanding more than asking for her to acquiesce. Claire found her arms winding around his neck as she leaned into his strength and parted her lips.

Fletch lifted her up, rucking the dress up around her waist. "Spread your legs and wrap them around me," he growled.

She would have liked to say he'd done something to force her, but he hadn't. She wanted him as much as he wanted her. Unbuttoning his fly, he removed his hard cock from his pants and as if it was a heat seeking missile, it found the entrance to her core and he thrust up into her, stretching and filling her as she moaned and held onto him.

"God, I missed you all day."

"You're the one who got up and left."

He shook his head. "What a brat. I should have known you weren't asleep. I won't make that mistake again. Next time, I'll either take you with me or leave you handcuffed to the bed with a security detail."

"Shut up and fuck me," she snarled.

Chuckling, he said, "Well, since you asked me so nice."

Holding her against the wall, he fucked her long and slow, never letting her get any purchase to do anything but let him have his way. The fact that 'his way' felt pretty damn amazing didn't hurt. Over and over, he surged up and then retreated. Every time she tried to wriggle away, he smacked her backside, never once changing the rhythm or power with which he stroked her.

"You feel so good," he groaned.

Each time he drove up into her, he pulled her down as well so that she was impaled on his cock down to the root. She couldn't move, couldn't get away from him, and she had to admit, if only to herself, that she didn't want to. Fletch was completely in control and in command and gave her no choice but to accept his dominance. He shoved himself deep until her entire body shook and her inner walls trembled. There was something about this man that just did something to her.

He held her up as he fucked her as if her weight was nothing. She felt dainty and utterly feminine in his strong embrace. Her muscles began to tighten as her breath became thready and his became ragged. Claire could no more have stopped her approaching orgasm than she could have stopped a speeding train. It crashed down around her as her pussy clamped down on his cock. He slammed into her a final time, as she writhed in his hold, and he flooded her with his cum.

Claire clung to Fletch as small tremors wracked her body afterwards, making her whimper as he made small movements still deep inside her, drawing tiny aftershocks from her.

"Go away," she whispered.

"Shh, Claire. Everything is going to be all right. I'm going to take care of you."

"No," she said, shaking her head.

"Yes," he crooned as he uncoupled from her and eased her back to her feet, pulling her close and steadying her.

"You searched my home," she accused him gently.

"And I found nothing. I also fed and watered your horses and mucked out your stalls. That ought to count for something."

"I suppose so. You'd better talk to the guy you had follow me into London this afternoon. He got lazy and I spotted him. I would have expected better from someone on your team."

Fletch stepped back, holding her separate from him. "I didn't have anyone trying to tail you, Claire. I didn't have to."

"Why not?"

"Because I put trackers in both pairs of your boots and those sandal thingies you had on when we had dinner at the Savoy. Who was following you?"

"I don't know. I thought it was you. Some guy in a black sedan. When I took him to Scotland Yard and the bobby looked like he might flag him down, he made a quick exit."

"Shit," he said, stuffing his cock back into his jeans, stepping away from her and buttoning his fly.

"Fletch, what is it?"

"That wasn't me or any of my team. Where did you pick up the tail?"

"Not far from here on the A2."

"Shit. They know who you are and where you live. You need to grab some things. Was Mia staying here with you for the weekend?" She nodded, wondering what had made him so agitated. It wasn't like where she lived was a big secret. "Get her things, as well. I'll have a couple of my guys come out and stay at your place to take care of the livestock."

"I've got neighbors who will do that."

He grabbed her upper arms and gave her a little shake. "Someone is after you. You do not want unarmed civilians who know nothing about what is going on to be anywhere around here. It's too dangerous."

She watched as he grabbed his phone and dialed, listening as he coolly and calmly gave orders, before turning her around and boosting her towards the stairs with a little swat. "Move it."

He took a slice of pizza, biting into it. "Holy shit, that's good." He glanced into the kitchen where he could see the pizza stone, mixing bowls, et cetera. "Did you make this?" he called to her as she got to the top of the stairs.

"Yes."

"Damn, you can cook?"

She laughed. "Yes."

Note to self: let a guy get laid and get some pizza in him and his disposition takes an upturn for the better. She grabbed both her and Mia's things, tucking them into the same large weekender bag. She had just reached the foot of the stairs when Fletch broadsided her with the grace and power of a large, predatory cat. He knocked the wind out of her momentarily as he flung her to the ground and a single shot was fired simultaneously through the window, hitting the thick wall panel where only moments before her head had been.

He hit two numbers on his phone and said, "Mayday! Mayday! We've been hit. Number of assailants and their positions unknown. I'm taking Claire upstairs. We'll hold them off until you can get here. Carter, keep going with Mia."

Claire grabbed his phone. "Belay that, or whatever it is you people say. I'm getting Fletch out of here. We'll be in my SUV. Mia will be able to answer questions."

She ended the call and handed him back the phone.

"That was stupid. We can't possibly get to your garage. The minute we step through one of those doors they'll cut us down. You can bet there's more than one of them out there."

"We're not going out any of those doors. Stay down and come with me."

CHAPTER 16

FLETCH

*C*laire crawled on her hands and knees towards the hidden doorway just beside the large kitchen pantry where she had a hutch that concealed her bolt hole and tunnel. She reached up with her hand, disengaged the alarm, and opened the door.

"You have got to be kidding me," he said with admiration. "That is not on the blueprints for your house."

She grinned at him. "Yeah, a couple of hefty bribes to my architect and contractor took care of that. Come on, let's get inside and get this door sealed behind us."

He followed her inside and watched as she closed the hatch—it was difficult to think of it as a door.

"How the fuck did they get so close? Carter had

some trouble getting past your perimeter alarm, and he's the best."

She managed to look sheepish. "Uh, I usually only leave the one on at the drive. I know Mia keeps telling me that's dumb, but everything sets the damn thing off—rabbits, hedgehogs, birds, the horses. I was racking up fines left and right…"

Claire re-engaged the alarm, and then attached a couple of wires to the mechanism.

"Do I want to know?" he asked.

A grin began to split her face and then got bigger. "Probably not, but I'll tell you anyway. If they find the latch—and that's a big if—whoever trips it is going to get a nasty shock. It won't kill the person, but it's got enough juice to knock them across the room."

"You're mean," he said, returning her grin. "It's surprisingly hot."

Claire rolled her eyes. "Come on, Romeo. Let's get the hell out of here."

She ran ahead of him down a set of stairs and into a tunnel he could tell she knew like the back of her hand. No flashlight or torch was needed. Claire reached back to take his hand, keeping him close and guiding him through the tunnel. They came up to the garage, and he pushed her behind him, taking his gun from the holster at the small of his back.

"You fucked me while packing a loaded gun?" He turned to look at her, nodding, and she grinned. "Surprisingly hot."

He shook his head, climbed the ladder up into the garage and looked around to make sure it was safe. Fletch beckoned her to his side and headed toward the SUV, which he noted had been backed in.

"Please tell me the keys are in there."

"And I filled up the tank just outside of town."

She was amazing. Most women he knew would be falling apart if they'd been shot at, but not Claire. Not only was she cool under pressure, but she almost looked like she was getting a kick out of it. Fletch knew he'd been developing a major thing for her—even thinking about a future with her—but he was beginning to believe it was so much more than that.

"I'm driving."

"I figured. I was going to give you shit about it, but I figure in this kind of situation, you're probably more experienced than me."

"Ya think? The way you operate, I doubt anyone's ever given chase, either by foot or by vehicle. Although I know of more than one dragnet that's been put out to catch you."

So, there it was, the proverbial elephant in the room.

"That's not all that impressive. They didn't know who to look for, only what."

He put her in the car and ran around to get in on the driver's side. Leaning over, he kissed her hard. "We're going to have a long talk about that," he said as he let her come up for air.

"That button," she said indicating the top button on the left of a set of two domino-like buttons with each domino having a green button and a red one. "Unlocks the garage and starts the doors to open. If you hit them at speed, they'll release and open up wide. This green button is for the front gate. It'll do the same thing. The two red buttons close the doors and the gate. If you don't press the button that unlocks them, you're not going to get through. I was assured that unless someone had a tank, they were crash proof."

"I can see we'll need to make some major improvements to my place in Devon."

"Beautiful farm you have. All that fresh sea air."

Had she just seen pictures or had she been there? She really was full of surprises. He hadn't thought to check her movements throughout the day, which he now understood had been foolish on his part.

Fletch hit the ignition switch and as the engine came to life, he hit the correct green button and floored it. He pressed between her shoulders forcing her to lean over.

"Stay down until I tell you otherwise." He was a bit surprised when he removed his hand, and she stayed in place.

The SUV's powerful motor sent the vehicle careening toward the doors, which, as Claire had told him, flew open the moment the bumper hit them. They'd caught the hit team unawares as it took them a moment to turn from the house and toward the SUV as he roared up Claire's drive to the highway.

One of the men got a shot off and it shattered the back window. High-powered ammo, just what they didn't need. He turned off the lights in the car to make them a harder target to hit. The night sky was overcast and there was no moon or stars to illuminate the road or fields. He could only barely make out the dirt road in front of him.

He glanced in the mirrors, which offered no help at all and chose to focus on the road ahead. She must have realized what he was thinking and turned the rearview mirror so she could use it to see behind them.

"I'll let you know if I see anything."

"Good girl."

She reached forward and hit the second button, two small lights on the ends of the gates lit up and gave him a great target to aim at as he shot out onto the road.

"Turn right."

"Greenwich and London are to the left."

"And so are a lot of innocent people, some of whom are my friends. What's the address of the safe-house. I assume we're heading there?"

"We are." He gave her the address and she pulled up the navigation system. "You have to be in park to enter an address."

"Not if your best friend is an electronics geek and

disabled that little safety feature. If Carter doesn't know how to do it for you, I can ask Mia."

"Don't be a brat, and don't set Carter and Mia against each other. I have a bad feeling we're going to have to get them to work together."

"If you can, keep the headlights off. Hopefully they'll head the other way. We can swing around on this backroad and then head in the right direction. I'm afraid Gertrude is going to cop an attitude."

"Gertrude?"

"Yeah, the nav unit. She gets pissy when you don't go where she wants. Once we're on the main highway and headed where she wants to go, she'll be fine."

Putting the pedal to the metal, he laughed. "I'm not sure I've ever had this much fun trying to outrun people trying to kill me."

She leaned back in her seat, perfectly relaxed. "Stick with me, Fletch. I can show you a real good time."

Of that, he had no doubt.

As much as he wanted to focus on her and make sure she was all right, he knew his job at this particular moment in time was to keep them on the road and out of the hands of whoever was trying to kill them. The leading contenders were Benito Petacci, the patriarch of the family; Sir Godfrey Robbins, who was terrified of something Claire knew; and Emil Franklin, the mysterious Swiss banker. Plenty of time to figure out who it was and neutralize the threat once he had her safe.

"See anything?" he asked.

"Not so far, but they could be keeping their headlights off as well. If they were as far behind us as I think, we may have gotten away clean."

"Let's not count on that. They didn't use vehicles to get to your millhouse. We have no idea where they parked. Keep using the mirrors to check."

"You do know it's too bloody dark to see anything, right?"

"Yeah, but it makes me feel better to know you're doing it."

Fletch floored the SUV, trying to get more speed. He was already doing eighty, which on these backroads with no headlights and no moon or stars seemed to be about the limit he could push. If he missed a turn or rolled the vehicle, he could kill them both.

He flexed his fingers around the steering wheel, tightening his grip. *Not on my watch.* He pushed for a little more speed, careening down the road. He needed to get them up on the highway. On these deserted backroads, there was no one who might see them, no bored cop looking to make a name for himself. It was just him and Claire; her life and future in his hands, and he meant to keep her safe.

"For what it's worth, Fletch?"

"Yeah?"

"When I think of all the men I've ever known, you're the only one for whom I would have ever considered walking away from my legacy."

"Your grandfather didn't leave you with a legacy; he left you with a damn millstone around your neck. What is it Sir Godfrey is afraid of?"

"Oh, that's a long and tawdry story. If we make it through the night, you can buy me breakfast at the Savoy, and I'll tell you all about it."

"Where's the damn necklace, Claire?"

"I'm sure I don't know what you're talking about," she said in a voice dripping with feigned innocence.

Fletch snorted. "Yeah, we're going to have a long talk about that, as well."

"You actually want to talk to me? And here I thought all you wanted to do was fuck."

He hazarded a glance in her direction and relaxed as he saw her grinning at him. She really was enjoying herself. "I can multi-task. How far are we from the main highway."

"Less than a mile. The road flows right onto the access road and then up onto the highway."

"My guess is if they have given chase, they're going to want to avoid those traffic cameras."

"Left here and then Gertrude should stop 'course correcting' and get us to your safehouse. Any chance we can stop for a burger? I had to leave my pizza behind and I'm hungry."

Fletch sneaked another glance. She really was

having a good time and it turned him on in a way nothing else had. She was baiting him—just for the fun of it. Well, two could play.

"I have to tell you the only decent burger in London is at the Savoy, but if we make it to the safehouse in one piece, I will personally grill you a burger that'll knock your socks off."

"Can I have cheese?"

He laughed. "Blue, cheddar, or pepperjack."

"Oooh, goodie. I'm a girl who likes choices. Do I get a choice of sleeping companions?"

Involuntarily he growled, which made her laugh. "Not a chance. You will no longer be sleeping alone or with anyone else. Got it?"

"Got it. I doubt any of them have as big a dick as yours."

"Baby, it ain't the size of the dick, it's what you can do with it."

That made her laugh uproariously. "Don't you believe it. It is most definitely the size of the dick. A girl can train a man how to use it, but no kind of miracle grow will make it any larger than the one your mama gave you."

As soon as they hit the highway, he turned his lights on and brought their speed back down to the speed limit before getting in the lane that would give him the maximum ability to maneuver to another lane, onto the shoulder or off the highway via an exit.

"So far, so good," she said taking a look in the mirror before positioning it so he could use it.

Fletch let the navigation system take them to the safehouse. After a while he felt safe enough to drive with one hand on the wheel and the other on the gear shift, with an eye to moving it further to the left to rest on her thigh. But before he could he felt her hand rest on top of his. His dick wanted her to move it further to the right so that her hand rested on top of it. But as he often said, his dick was a greedy bastard, and he would just have to settle for the sweetness of the gesture she'd made in wanting to reestablish a connection with him.

Finally, they pulled into the drive of the safehouse and made their way down to what had once been a cloister for nuns up through World War II. It had then been turned into a hospital and when the war was over, it had been left to lie and await a new purpose—a secure safehouse for his team and anyone needing their protection.

He would need to tell the team in the morning that their mission had switched from retrieving the necklace to keeping Mia and Claire safe. He would negotiate with the authorities, the insurance companies and those they'd robbed, but as of tonight, Claire and Mia were out of the vigilante justice business.

Mia came barreling out of the house as they pulled up, launching herself at Claire.

Fletch looked at Carter. "Next time, she doesn't

leave the house until you've made sure we're still secure."

"What the fuck happened?" asked Joe Baxter, his second in command. He'd been with Fletch during the war, and when his tour had been up, he'd joined his old commander's fledgling security firm.

"Someone sent a hit squad. They were well-armed and well-prepared. If it hadn't been for Claire and her escape tunnel, I'm not sure we could have held them off until the cavalry arrived."

Claire wrapped her arm around Mia, and they headed into the house. He caught up with them and disengaged Claire from Mia, who he thrust at Carter.

"Get her back inside and see that she stays there." He watched them return to the abbey and detained Claire until they were alone. "All that shit back in the SUV about burgers and the like?"

She took his face in her hands and kissed him deeply. "I knew all I had to do was turn it over to you and you'd get us to safety. I figured I'd just lighten the mood. I never doubted you for a minute. How about you find us a bed and fuck me into oblivion?"

Realizing she was barefoot, he scooped her up into his arms and carried her into the house. It seemed his night was far from over, but he could handle this. There would be a lot to figure out come morning, but for right now, Claire was safe here with him, but more importantly, in his arms and headed for his bed.

CHAPTER 17

CLAIRE

From the moment he'd trusted her to get them out of the millhouse right up until he'd lifted her into his arms as if she weighed nothing, she'd felt safe, protected, and cherished. Poppi had always made her feel loved, but he'd wanted her strong and capable. She'd known he felt somehow responsible for her parents' death, and she had suspected Sir Godfrey, or someone close to him, had something to do with it, although he'd never struck her as a killer. But why on earth would he have wanted to kill her parents or Poppi for that matter?

"Are you with me Claire? Are you in shock? Are you hungry?" Fletch asked, his voice filled with concern.

"Huh?"

"I asked if you were hungry."

"I thought we covered that outside. I want you

and your big dick in a bed and fucking me until I've screamed this place down around your ears and fall asleep exhausted with you still deep inside me. Any questions?"

The small group of men and Mia who had been creating a general buzz from people checking with each other and making sure they were secure went silent.

"That goes for the rest of you," she said. "Well, not the fucking me or big dicks, but does anyone at all have any questions about what it is I want?"

"No, brat, I think you've made that perfectly clear," Fletch said, heading up the stairs with laughter and catcalls floating up from the main floor.

"Let me guess," she teased, "another thing we're going to have a long talk about…"

He kicked open the door to the main bedroom, carried her through and then kicked it closed behind him. "Let me be very clear. Our talk? That's going to mostly be me telling you how it is and you agreeing to behave yourself and do as you're told."

"Oh, that doesn't sound like me at all."

"It's the new you."

"But I thought you liked me just the way I am?"

Why was it men always wanted to change women? What they found fun and exciting in a casual or new girlfriend, they soon wanted to mold into some boring version of her when things got more serious.

"I like you just the way you are, but you cannot

continue living the way you have been."

"Why not? I'm perfectly happy doing what I do. You can put me down now."

"I don't think I will. I find you listen better when my cock is shoved up deep inside you."

"Fuck you," she spat at him, really wanting to get down.

"That's on the agenda, baby. Settle down."

"No."

"What is wrong with you?"

"Not one damn thing. I thought we were getting along…"

"We are," he said, his voice filled with exasperation as he set her down on her feet.

She spun out of his arms and glared at him. She knew her eyes had to be flashing. Poppi had always said she was typical 'black Irish' in both looks and temper. Was she always to be a disappointment to the men in her life—not thin enough, not rich enough, not pliable enough?

"Not really. We fuck a couple of times and suddenly you go all caveman—me Tarzan, you Jane."

"Tarzan wasn't a caveman. Did you miss the part where somebody sent a hit squad after you? Do you understand you and Mia would have been killed?"

"Me? What about you? I'm sure a man in your position makes lots of enemies. And what makes you so damn sure they didn't follow you? We were in the house; we had homemade pizza and were going to watch a couple of movies, and then you and Hawkman barge in..."

"Hawkman?"

"Yeah. You know, Carter Hall? Hawkman from *DC Comics Legends of Tomorrow?*"

"What the fuck are you talking about?" he asked, confusion written all over his face.

"Your tech guy is named after a superhero."

"He is?"

She shook her head. "I don't want to fight with you, and I'm not changing anything about me for you. If you don't want to fuck me, just say so. I'll either find someone who does or do without, although I was really looking forward to another go round with your dick."

His eyes flashed with anger and his skin took on a ruddy hue. "So, any dick in a storm will do?"

Claire straightened her spine. "You don't get to be jealous. And yeah, any dick that doesn't want me to give up what my whole life has been about. Know anyone?"

"Your whole life hasn't been about you being a jewel thief."

"Yes, it has. Every single fucking thing I've ever done in my life has been geared to one goal and one goal only—to right the wrongs made not only by the Nazis but by a group of unscrupulous men who decided it was better to steal from those they didn't think could do anything about it."

"There are legal ways to do these things."

"Are you so fucking naive that you truly believe that? My grandfather did that—tried going up the chain of command. Sir Godfrey's father and his cronies got him cashiered. It changed the entire trajectory of his life. He went to prison."

"Sir Godfrey's father was dealing in stolen Nazi treasure?"

"Hot news flash, he and his buddies were doing some of the stealing, but yes, they took jewelry, art, and anything they could get their greedy little hands on to make themselves richer."

He sat down on the edge of the bed—everything about him saying 'defeated.' He ran his hands through his hair.

"This is going to be so much more difficult than I thought," he said.

"What is going to be 'difficult?' I get it. You don't think I'm good enough as I am, so you want to change me. I don't want to change. So, it isn't 'difficult,' it's impossible. Why don't you just close your eyes for a minute, I'll go through the window, down the wall, and disappear. Could you take care of Mia? You're right; it's probably getting too dangerous for her. Tell them I blackmailed her into helping me."

"Did you?" he said, looking up at her with a stark expression.

"Of course, not. What kind of bitch do you think I am?"

He stood up and took her hand, trying to draw her back to him. "I don't think you're a bitch at all. I said 'difficult,' not 'impossible,' and you're not going anywhere."

"Well, I'm sure as hell not staying here with you."

"My big dick really wishes you'd stop saying that. It's getting very concerned that you might actually mean what you say, and it was really, really looking forward to getting back up inside you."

She couldn't help but smile at him. He had a way of being as completely inappropriate as she was. No, he wasn't inappropriate, he could act it on occasion when it suited him. But Ryland Fletcher was a straight arrow. He had a clearly defined sense of right and wrong and lived in a world where black was black and white was white. Her entire life had been spent in a morally gray area.

"Well, I'm afraid your dick is going to have to live with disappointment." She let go and stepped back. "Seriously, this thing—whatever it is—will never work between us."

"It will if we want it to. And I, for one, want it to —perhaps more than anything else I've ever wanted. Let's go to bed, baby. We're both tired and wrung out. It's been a long night. We'll figure it out in the morning."

"Don't get me wrong. I would really like to go to bed with you. I'd like nothing better than to fuck you, go to sleep, and wake up in a world where we could be together. But I'm too much of a realist. We can't."

"We can. I can and will make a world where we can be together. I could have gone to the Yard with everything my team and I have on you, but I haven't. The last thing I want is to see you or Mia get arrested. It's just going to take a little more negotiating than I thought, but that isn't to say I won't get it done."

She shook her head. "You just don't get it. I don't want you to get anything done, not if it means I have to walk away from everything I've worked for."

"It isn't everything. It's a burden your grandfather saddled you with."

Claire's hand cracked across his cheek before the thought to slap him had even fully formed in her mind. "Don't you ever talk about Poppi that way. He gave up everything to take care of me. He worked for a family that he loathed."

She thought he'd get angry, maybe even lash out at her verbally, but he didn't. Instead, he folded her in his arms, and just held her.

"I think your grandfather was an extraordinary man, and I wish he was around to help me put an end to this vendetta you seem committed to, but he isn't. I think it must have cost him to walk away from something he must have believed in every bit as deeply as you do and work for people he despised to give you a better life. But he saw the greater good—keeping his granddaughter safe. I think he would want me to do the same. And to do that, you have to say enough is enough. I also think if he thought this could get you killed, he would have put a stop to it. It wasn't me they were after tonight; it was you, and Mia, to a lesser extent."

"You don't know that," she said, her cheek pressed hard to his chest.

Placing his crooked finger under her chin, he tilted her head back. "But I do, and so do you. Come to bed, Claire. We'll figure it out in the morning."

He fell back onto the bed, bringing her with him. She struggled only for a moment, but her heart wasn't in it. Every scrap of her soul wanted to be with this man—wanted to believe they could be together forever, but she didn't. Too much had gone before them and created an insurmountable divide between who they were, but tonight, that didn't matter.

Someone had tried to kill her. Mia would have just been collateral damage. She'd known for a while she would need to find a way to protect Mia, and now she had one. The Grenadine Necklace was lost to her and those to whom it truly belonged. She knew that now. She could never return to her beloved millhouse. She knew she could trust Fletch to deal with all of it—the stolen jewelry, her horses, the paintings she'd been working on, Mia. It was time for Claire Mitchell to disappear and lay low for a while. Then she could re-emerge and strike at those who had cost so many everything they had.

Claire knew she should send him away or sneak out when he wasn't paying attention. She could ply him with sex, make him believe he could have what he wanted and then just slip away like the proverbial thief in the night. But she wanted him one last time. There would never be another Fletch—someone who challenged her, wanted the best for her and could make her body and soul come alive in a way it never had and wouldn't do again. The bittersweet knowledge of what had to be clutched at her heart. She would give herself this final time and then mourn his loss for the rest of her days.

Somehow, during her musings, he had stripped them both naked and had positioned her on her back as he moved down her body, spreading her thighs to expose her sex as he lowered his head to her, kissing and licking her clit and her labia. Claire moaned and gave herself to him this one last time.

Her body was soft and yielding and her pussy slick and ready for him. He latched onto her with his mouth, feasting on her honey as he plunged his tongue inside her over and over, lapping up all she could give him. Her body bowed as she came, gasping and shaking as she did.

"You are so fucking beautiful. I can make this right. Tell me you believe me."

"I believe you." She didn't, but he didn't need to know that.

He stretched down, lowering his body to hers and

making a place for himself between her legs. His hands slid under her ass, and he held her as he watched her intently. "Say it again," he said as he slid his hard length inside her, pressing deep so they were joined together.

"I believe," she moaned, and for that one exquisite moment when he was buried in her as deeply as he could be, she did.

He kissed her as he drew back, then kissed her again as he thrust home. Over and over, he repeated his actions until they had established the same rhythm they had found before. Claire cherished each word, each touch, each sigh, committing them to memory so she would have them to sustain her for the rest of her life. She would take this night with him and leave the only man she'd ever loved to deal with the fallout. It wasn't the noble or honorable thing to do, but it was what had to be.

Again and again, he moved forward and back. She felt the orgasm as it bloomed throughout her and she tightened around him, softly calling his name. He drove forward hard until he was pressed to his root as his cock began pumping his cum inside her, bathing her inner walls with his warmth.

He collapsed onto her, his weight pushing her down into the soft mattress. She wanted to stay there forever. But forever was a dream she couldn't allow herself to believe.

CHAPTER 18

FLETCH

*T*he morning dawned and a very sleepy, very sated Claire was curled up in his arms with her head on his chest. His last thought from the night before had been to get her on her back and slip back into her before she was even awake. He wanted her too tired and snuggly to argue with him. He knew what she believed he was asking her to give up, but there was no other way.

She rubbed her cheek against his chest, a small smile playing across her lips. She wasn't really awake. He still had time to enact his master plan of keeping her so invested in being with him and his big dick that she could let go of her grandfather's obsession and let it join him in his grave. That didn't mean he wasn't going to bring to light the sketchy provenance and anything Claire might have to prove where the remaining stolen jewelry really belonged, but she needed him to take care of it.

"Fletch," she began, raising herself up on her elbow.

He pressed her back down. "Don't start, Claire. Just let it be, at least until I've made love to you again."

When had fucking her become making love? He didn't know and didn't care; he just knew and accepted that it had.

Just as he nudged her onto her back and slipped his hand between her legs, there was a knock on the door. "Fletch?" called Carter from the other side.

Claire groaned. "Make him go away."

"Would Mia go away if she thought she'd found something you needed?"

She whined a little, and he chuckled.

"Can't you just shoot him or something?"

"I can but he'd be hard to replace."

"Then shoot one of the others as a warning."

He laughed and kissed her. God, he loved kissing Claire Mitchell. Normally, he didn't like kissing. It felt awkward and far too intimate. He supposed it said everything about who she was becoming to him that it felt as though they'd been doing it for years, and he welcomed the intimacy.

"That wouldn't do much to build team loyalty and cohesiveness," he said as he rolled off the bed, not bothering to get dressed before opening the door.

If someone was going to force him to leave a compliant and aroused Claire in bed, they were just going to have to deal with his erection. Opening the door, he was surprised to find not only Carter, but Mia.

"She wouldn't settle down and go to bed last night, so we've been going through everything."

"Tell him if his dick was big enough, he could have used that. Trust me, Mia would have been putty in his hands."

"My dick is more than big enough..." called Carter before realizing what he'd said.

"It is?" asked Mia. "Want to show me?"

"See? I told you she likes big dicks. In general, girls like big dicks." Claire was on a roll.

"That's enough out of you," Fletch said. "Hush."

He turned back to Carter, who was still blushing. He felt Claire press her warm, naked body to his back, wrapping her arms around him.

"Why don't you two go downstairs, and we'll join you in a minute. Whatever it is can wait until Claire and I get dressed."

"I don't know that it can," started Mia.

Fletch blocked her from entering their bedroom. He was going to make a rule about not waking them up unless it was imminent life and death, and no one entered their space without an express invitation from him. Carter really should have done something with

Mia to put her in a better mood. He'd have to have a talk with him about that.

"Tell her to go away," he said to Claire.

"You told me to hush."

Fletch laughed. He did that a lot around Claire. She was good for him. She thought he saw things in terms of black and white—dark and light. She was wrong. He only saw darkness. He supposed that wasn't technically true. He'd only seen the darkness before he met her. She had brought him the light; she was his light—a shining beacon illuminating the endless possibilities for joy.

"So, now you decide you want to do what you're told?"

"He knows more than he's saying," said Mia.

"You're wrong about him," said Carter.

"No, I'm not. You and he and all of the rest of them are just part of the system. You're all a part of what we've been fighting against."

"No, they're not."

He couldn't keep himself from smiling. He loved how she defended him without a lot of bullshit. Just three little words that meant the world to him.

"Carter, take Mia back downstairs. If we need to gather the team, do that and have someone start breakfast. Claire and I will be down in a minute."

Mia started to say something, but Carter manned up and did what was needed: turning her away and giving her backside a little swat. This might work out better than he'd planned. He could leave Carter in charge of Mia and her technology, and he could focus on Claire and making her happy. Closing the door, he turned within the circle of her arms.

"I don't suppose I can persuade you that we need to fuck before we go back downstairs, can I?" she said, looking sexier than anyone had a right to.

"I wish. When we can get a little breathing space, how about you and I go somewhere with warm, sandy beaches and kick out the cobwebs with a nice gallop along the shoreline."

"I always feel so sorry for those horses. They never look like they've been fed all that well. How about we go to your place in Devon and gallop glorious horses along a rugged coastline before we fuck all day?"

"But then we can't order room service."

"Room service is way overrated. I'll cook."

"I prefer you naked."

"So, I won't fry bacon," she said mischievously.

She really was a brat, and there was no more room for doubt, he wasn't just crazy about her, he was madly in love with her.

"I think I can arrange for that to happen, but first, I need to get you out of this mess you, Mia, and your grandfather created." She pulled away, and he let her go as he held up his hand to stop her from defending her grandfather. "This may surprise you, but I think your grandfather and I would have gotten along splendidly."

Claire laughed ruefully. "I don't think you could be more wrong. You and Poppi are nothing alike."

"Maybe, but we would have had one very big thing in common." She raised her eyebrows in silent question. "We both loved his granddaughter, and that one thing would have made the rest pale in comparison."

He kissed her to keep from hearing her protest. Claire was going to take a lot of patience. The only person she'd ever been anything to was her grandfather and he had been dead for a long time. It was going to take reassuring her again and again that she was everything to him before she believed it.

"I think I have a way to fix it so you can walk away and not have to worry about someone trying to kill you. I have contacts with Lloyd's, the Yard, and a lot of other places. I've never given away anything that would allow them to connect you or Mia to any of this. Hell, I've never even connected the dots for them, so they don't see the pattern. No one knows your or Mia's name."

"Then how do you explain my sudden appearance in your life."

"The horses. You're a top equestrienne, and I breed top sport horses. You are an art restoration expert and appraiser. A great deal of my business involves recovering losses in the art world. Anybody thinking about it will see it was inevitable we'd run into each other. And when they see our chemistry, they won't doubt that we're anything but two people in love…"

"I never said I loved you," she said, interrupting him.

"No, but you do."

There it was, the other big elephant in the room. Both were truths: she was a master jewel thief, and they were in love with each other.

"I can fix this, Claire. I can make it all go away, and we can right the wrongs your grandfather devoted his life to up until you came along. He stopped once you were in the picture, didn't he? That's why there's a break in the pattern, and why no one connected them."

"He didn't stop at first—not until I found his stash and he had to tell me what he was doing and why."

He nodded. "I wondered if it wasn't something like that. None of that matters. I can keep your grandfather out of it, as well. But you need to believe me. You need to trust me. I can fix all of this. I just need the Grenadine Necklace and whatever else you haven't disposed of."

"It's not that simple."

"It is, if you trust me. The insurance companies just want the jewelry back. The cops just want the thefts to stop. When you walk away, we'll make sure there's nothing to connect back to you and Mia. I'll persuade Lloyd's to remove the bounty from your head. Once they withdraw their money and support, the rest will follow. Trust me, Claire, we can have the life we want."

"How am I supposed to trust you when you refuse to understand…"

He drew her back in his arms. "I do understand. I understand what drove your grandfather, and I understand he passed that legacy on to you. But it doesn't have to take over your life. Even your grandfather walked away when he realized it would hurt you."

"You can have everything but the Grenadine Necklace."

He shook his head. "No, baby, you made the Grenadine Necklace too showy. It was all over the news. The insurance companies need to save face, and recovering the Grenadine Necklace allows them to do that."

"Do you know its history?"

"You mean about Mussolini and Clara Petacci? Yes, I know. But her descendants are not only huge clients of Lloyd's but also of the biggest insurance company in Switzerland and one of the Swiss banks. Yeah, I know, and I get it."

"I don't know that you do. Poppi believed that Sir Godfrey's father had my parents killed. The old bastard was so invested in making sure what he did never saw the light of day that he forced them off the road. It's a miracle I wasn't killed. Poppi forced Sir Godfrey to take him on as his horse master and driver. Part of his compensation was a place for us to live and for me to have everything their ill-gotten gains had given Evangeline."

"Trust me, you are way out of Evangeline's league, and I mean that in a good way."

She looked as if he'd slapped her in the face. "You know Evangeline?"

"I used to."

"Does she know about Mia and me?"

"No. We broke up more than a year and a half ago. I hadn't even started putting the pieces together."

"You and Evangeline were together? You didn't think to share that little bit of information with me, and you expect me to trust you?"

"You're going into a jealous snit over a woman I haven't seen in more than eighteen months? I could never understand the jealousy she had about the horse master's daughter. But I get it now." He laughed. "She always referred to you as the 'chubby urchin' or the 'chubby ragamuffin.' For the record you are neither chubby, an urchin, or a ragamuffin. In her dreams. She doesn't have your luscious curves, bold spirit. and keen mind. She doesn't hold a candle to you, but then, I suspect she knows that. She hates you, by the way."

"Trust me, the feeling is mutual."

"None of that is important."

"It is to me."

"Quit behaving like a child and listen to me. The most important thing is your and Mia's safety and extricating you from this nasty web you've entangled yourselves in. Babe, I need to know where the Grenadine Necklace and the rest of the stash are." She shook her head. "Don't tell me no, Claire; we will find it."

She laughed, the sound bitter instead of her usual joyful noise. "You tried the other morning and never even came close." She laughed again. "That's not true. You were so close to the Grenadine Necklace. I had it in my pillowcase. It isn't there now, but you had no idea how close you were."

He watched as her open face and body posture began to shut down. She was trying to cast him in the role of the bad guy, so she didn't have to admit she loved him; admit that they belonged together and walk away from everything she'd known. It was a big ask and he knew it, but he would make sure she was safe, no matter what.

"Come take a shower with me, Claire. Let me show you how good having a positive dominant male in your life can be."

"I'm not sure I'm ready for another round with you and your big dick."

He chuckled. "It's time you learned I'm good for more than my abilities with my big dick."

Fletch dragged Claire, only semi-protestingly into the shower. He fisted her hair, tugging her head back and brushing her lips with his. His cock came back online with her naked body so close to his. He'd never believed he could feel this way about anyone, much less someone he hadn't known all that long. Maybe that was a good thing. This way they'd have more of their lives to spend together. Well, as long as he could keep her from getting herself killed.

She was the most beautiful, sexy, sensual, intelligent woman he'd ever known. She was his lighthouse that kept him from the jagged rocks and pointed him toward safe harbor. He grabbed the large, natural sea sponge and the soap. Once the sponge was warm and soapy, he began to wash the excesses of the past few nights from her body.

His cock, or big dick as she liked to call it, throbbed between them. It would have to wait. Claire didn't need another orgasm or three. What she needed was his focus and reassurance.

"That feels good," she moaned, leaning back into his strength.

"You feel good, right," he whispered nuzzling her neck, just behind the ear, loving the way her whole body seemed to light up.

The soapy sponge moved down her body, circling her breasts before driving between her legs and brushing her clit. She sighed contentedly. Claire seemed to love it when he played in or around her pussy, which was good, because he planned to spend a lot of time doing it.

As soon as he got things arranged, he intended to spend whole days doing nothing more than fucking and caring for her in all ways. His cock got painfully hard and Fletch was sure it was beginning to make plans of its own.

Much as he didn't want to, Fletch turned down the temperature of the water and rinsed the soap from her body before quickly washing his own. He helped her out of the shower, and began to gently pat her down, drying every inch of her until she was warm through and through.

Finding sweatpants and a tank top for her, he marveled at how incredibly sexy she looked. His woman was a bombshell—no doubt about it—in more ways than one. Now to see about getting the bomb defused before it blew up in their faces.

CHAPTER 19

CLAIRE

Fletch spent the rest of the day in London doing heavy negotiations to get both Claire and Mia clear of any allegations that might result from the return of her 'pirate booty,' as he'd termed it. Carter and one other man were with him, just in case, as Claire had hypothesized at breakfast, the hit team had been after him and Carter and not her and Mia.

It was early afternoon and she and Mia were standing in front of the wall of windows that led out onto an enormous deck overlooking the valley below. They had been informed that it was hurricane and bullet proof glass that was rated to withstand a Category 5 hurricane and the fire power of an Apache attack helicopter, so they felt safe standing there.

"You're not staying, are you?" said Mia, choking back quiet tears.

"I can't. I'm too much of a liability to all of you. Stick close to Fletch and Carter. They'll make sure you're okay. In fact, ask Fletch for a job. You'd be good at this. You and Carter make a good team."

"So do you and Fletch."

"I won't deny that. I'll even let you in on a little secret, last night he told me he loved me. I couldn't tell him because I wasn't sure of him or what a future with him might look like. Now I know. I love him, Mia." She heard her friend catch a breath. "I love him so much it hurts. There will never be anyone but Fletch for me."

"Claire, there must be a way. At least let me come with you."

"It won't work. I need to focus on my mission and having you along will distract me from that. Besides, I need you here to open a window in the security system so I can get away."

"I can't talk you out of this?"

Claire took Mia's hand in hers and squeezed it. She'd never felt so alone.

"I found some sneakers, and I'll head straight to our drop point. Take Fletch and the guys to the mill-house. Give them what we have in the way of jewels as well as all the documentation we found on their true ownership. Ask Fletch to take care of my horses. Sell the millhouse and keep the proceeds. I left you a power of attorney in the safe."

Mia inhaled with a short, sharp stab of breath.

"You're never coming back." It wasn't a question, just a statement of fact.

"I think it's best. Give me ten minutes to get what I need from upstairs. I'll leave Fletch a note. Watch over him for me, Mia. And be happy with Carter."

"Carter and I aren't involved…"

"Yet," Claire teased. "The operative word is 'yet.' I have loved three people in my life that I can remember: Poppi, Fletch, and you. Be happy, and now let me get out of here before I become a snotty mess with red, swollen eyes."

Claire drew away and trotted up the stairs, each step taking her away from the only two living people she'd ever loved. Time to rejoin Poppi and complete their mission.

FLETCH

"What do you mean she's gone," Fletch roared at the men he'd left behind to safeguard his life, knowing full well they weren't to blame. He turned to the one person he knew had helped her, Mia. "Where is she?

"I don't know," stammered Mia, sinking back against Carter.

"Tell him," said Carter.

"I don't know. All I know is that she believes she is on some kind of holy mission…"

"She's not," growled Fletch, getting a rein on his temper. Scaring the shit out of Mia was going to do nothing to improve the situation. "Tell me what I need to know to find her and keep her safe. I've made a deal with all parties involved. The Petacci's will withdraw their insurance claim and cease trying to find Claire in exchange for the return of the Grenadine Necklace. Lloyd's will cease and desist any and all attempts to bring the thief to justice, in return for the jewels still in your stash. Between the two, the bounty on her head will fall apart, and no one will have added impetus to find her, but I have to know where she is."

"It isn't that I won't tell you. I don't know. I know where the stash is, and I know that she left you a note upstairs. I can also grant you access to a secure chatroom on the dark web. It's a dead drop. You can leave her a note, but that's about it."

Fletch pinched the bridge of his nose. "I'm getting a terrible headache. Text me the IP address of the chatroom. Take the boys to the stash and bring it back here. I'll go upstairs and see what the brat has to say."

He opened the door of the bedroom. He could feel her loss in this room as keenly as he'd felt it when he entered the house. He'd known Claire was gone before he saw the faces of his people or before anyone had spoken a single word.

Fletch looked at the bed. The note, in her bold handwriting, couldn't have been more obvious had it been a coiled snake. He snatched it up and flipped it open.

> Fletch,
>
> For what it's worth—and I know that may not be much at this point—I love you. But the day I buried my grandfather, I made him a vow that I would carry on his work and restore as much of the jewels and treasure that the Nazis and their collaborators—both formal and hidden—had stolen to their rightful owners.
>
> Mia will take you to our cache of things we've already liberated. She will also show you the evidence we have that should see these things returned not to those who filed an insurance claim, but to those for whom they are priceless.
>
> Please know that nothing and no one could have taken me away from you save the one man who loved me first. I owe him. I owe him a debt I can never repay. I'm choosing to break my heart in sacrifice to that debt and hope someday you will find a way to forgive me and move on.
>
> I love you.

Claire

Damn it, Claire. Why couldn't you believe in us and trust me to take care of this?

His phone buzzed. He knew it wasn't her. He pulled it from his pocket and looked at the IP address, pressing the link to take him to the chatroom where they had kept in contact with their various couriers and those to whom they had returned a part of their families' histories.

He thought about making it an encrypted message for her alone but decided to let those whom she believed she served see what she had done. He started to write a long note, pointing out all the ways he could make this right and begging her to come back to him. Then he thought about her defense of him earlier in the day. He decided to follow her lead: succinct and to the point.

> Claire, I love you. I will find you and bring you home. Fletch and his big dick

$\sim$

Thank you for reading To Love A Thief. The conclusion happens in My Fair Thief.

Deception and betrayal always carry a

price, sooner or later, someone has to pay.

Claire was determined Fletch would not be the one who paid the price. Running was her only option. On the run Claire has been hiding, not staying anywhere long, trying to find who wants her dead. When Fletch finds her she has no choice but to reveal her secrets in order to protect him. Someone is trying to kill them both and keep her grandfather's secrets from ever seeing the light of day.

When Fletch gives her an ultimatum, him or the next heist, her hesitation angers him. He is risking both his life and career to keep her safe. By the time she makes her decision, Claire has run out of options... her best friend's life is on the line.

Will Claire and Fletch survive this deadly game of cat and mouse?

With heart-pounding action, edge of your seat suspense and a steamy romance that heats every page, My Fair Thief is a must read for fans of romantic suspense.

ALSO BY DELTA JAMES

Contemporary Suspense

Relentless Pursuit (Duet)

Club Southside (spinoff Mercenary Masters)

Mercenary Masters

Wild Hearts

<u>Stealing her Heart</u>

<u>Claiming Her Heart</u>

<u>Taming her Heart</u>

<u>Finding her Heart</u>

Wild Mustang

<u>Hampton</u>

<u>Mac</u>

<u>Croft</u>

<u>Noah</u>

<u>Thom</u>

<u>Reid</u>

Crooked Creek Ranch

<u>Taming His Cowgirl</u>

<u>Tamed on the Ranch</u>

Paranormal Suspense

Mystic River Shifters (small town shifter)

<u>Defiant Mate</u>

<u>Savage Mate</u>

Reckless Mate

Shameless Mate

Runaway Mate

Otter Cover Shifters (small town shifters/ spinoff Mystic River)

Suspicious Mate

Unexpected Mate

Syndicate Masters

Midwest

Kiss of Luck

Stroke of Fortune

Twist of Fate

Eastern Seaboard

High Stakes

High Roller

High Bet

La Cosa Nostra

Ruthless Honor

Feral Oath

Defiant Vow

Northern Lights

Alliance

Complication

Judgment

Syndicate Masters

The Bargain

The Pact

The Agreement

The Understanding

The Pledge

Box Set

Looking Glass Multiverse

Shifted Reality

Shifted Existence

Shifted Dimension

Box Set

Reign of Fire

Dragon Storm

Dragon Roar

Dragon Fury

Masters of Valor (spin off Masters of the Savoy)

Prophecy

Illusion

Deception

Inheritance

Masters of the Savoy

Advance

Negotiation

Submission

Contract

Bound

Release

Ghost Cat Canyon

Determined

Untamed

Bold

Fearless

Strong

Fated Legacy (spin-off Tangled Vines)

Touch of Fate

Touch of Darkness

Touch of Light

Touch of Fire

Touch of Ice

Touch of Destiny

Tangled Vines (spin-off Wayward Mates)

Corked

Uncorked

Decanted

Breathe

Full Bodied

Late Harvest

Mulled Wine

Wayward Mates

In Vino Veritas

Brought to Heel

Marked and Mated

Mastering His Mate

Taking His Mate

Claimed and Mated

Claimed and Mastered

Hunted and Claimed

Captured and Claimed

Alpha Lords

Warlord

Overlord

Wolflord

Fated

Dragonlord

Co-writes

Masters of the Deep

Silent Predator

Fierce Predator

Savage Predator

Wicked Predator

Deadly Predator

ABOUT THE AUTHOR

Other books by Delta James: <ins>https://www.</ins> <ins>deltajames.com/</ins>

As a USA Today bestselling romance author, Delta James aims to captivate readers with stories about complex heroines and the dominant alpha males who adore them. For Delta, romance is more than just a love story; it's a journey with challenges and thrills along the way.

After creating a second chapter for herself that was dramatically different than the first, Delta now resides in Florida where she relaxes on warm summer evenings with her loveable pack of basset hounds as they watch the birds, squirrels and lizards. When not crafting fast-paced tales, she enjoys horseback riding, walks on the beach, and white-water rafting.

Delta loves connecting with her readers and tries to respond personally to as many messages as she can! You can find her on Facebook https://www.facebook. com/DeltaJamesAuthor and in her reader group https://www.facebook.com/groups/ 348982795738444.

ACKNOWLEDGMENTS

Thank you to my Patreon supporters.
I couldn't do this without you!

Carol Chase
Latoya McBride
Julia Rappaport
D F
Ellen
Margaret Bloodworth
Tamara Crooks
Rhonda
Autumn
Suzy Sawkins
Cindy Vernon
Linda Kniffen-Wager
Karen Somerville

Printed in Great Britain
by Amazon

22873605R00138